Cyberpunk City
Book One
The Machine Killer

D.L. Young

No part of this book may be reproduced in any form or by any electronic or mechanical means - except in the case of brief quotations embodied in articles or reviews - without the written permission of the author.

The characters and events portrayed in this book are fictitious. Any similarity to real persons, living or dead or undead or even just hanging on in a coma, is purely coincidental and not intended by the author.

Cover art by Ignacio Bazan-Lazcano

For free books, new release updates, exclusive previews and content, visit dlyoungfiction.com

The greatest crimes in the world are not committed by people breaking the rules but by people following the rules.

— Banksy

1
CATCHING FIREFLIES

They had no idea he was stalking them.

Blackburn Maddox watched the three intruders from a distance, the zoom on his avatar maxed out. They looked like a trio of fireflies buzzing next to some enormous block of light, seduced by its luminosity, ignorant of the approaching danger. He closed the distance slowly, careful to avoid detection. A predator creeping up on unaware prey.

They were newbies—probably just kids. Wannabe data thieves. Two of them seemed pretty clueless at first glance, their avatars bouncing off each other and jerking about, barely under the control of their users. The third was a bit less clueless, though still far from skilled. Just a bit less twitchy than his buddies. Maddox would have to keep his eye on that one.

He'd have to nail them quickly, before they got any farther or, God forbid, managed to make a critical breach. Even wannabe datajackers got lucky sometimes.

"Christ, man, are you just going to sit there and watch them break into R&D?" Maddox started at the

1

disembodied voice of one of the directors. Reflexively, he glanced around, but of course there was no one there. The two directors weren't plugged into virtual space with him. They were sitting next to him in the conference room, sipping coffee from cups and watching his avatar's POV on a holo monitor.

He'd already forgotten their names, referring to them inwardly as dickhead one and dickhead two.

"Just so we're clear," dickhead one said, "you fuck this up and it's your ass, not ours. You understand that, right?" The executive uttered the warning with the same indifferent tone Maddox imagined the man had used when ordering his latte.

"Yeah, I got it," Maddox answered. Shit flowed downhill at Latour-Fisher Biotechnologies, just like it did everywhere else.

But it was a good job, he reminded himself, and he was lucky to have it. The last thing he wanted to do was mess it up.

Still, he couldn't help picturing the kids on the other end of those avatars. Dumb and reckless, full of hormones and teen bravado, ready to take on the world. He'd been there, half a lifetime ago, pulling his share of stupid stunts in his early datajacking days. Okay, maybe more than his share.

But even back then, as green and naive as he was, he'd known the consequences of getting busted, known the price he'd have to pay. And these three little fireflies surely knew it too.

Sorry, kids. You picked the wrong house to rob today.

Maddox breathed in deeply and focused on his task, letting his body, his meat sack, slip further away, immersing his awareness into virtual space. He pulled up the sniffer trace he'd tagged the three intruders with earlier. An image appeared, hovering beside him, visible only to him and the two dickheads watching on the monitor. At first it visualized as a softly glowing orb, displaying the whole of the world, then as it sped through its routines, narrowing the search, the orb flattened into a 2D map. The western hemisphere zoomed into the Americas, then North America. A moment later it focused on the Northeastern US, on the wide swath of the City at the center of the image.

So they were local boys.

He turned his attention back to the firefly avatars, still darting back and forth anxiously. Boys, definitely. Most likely early teens. He could tell by the way they moved about. To anyone else they looked like jittery, bobbing pinpoints of light, but he knew better.

"They're picking the lock," dickhead two blurted, his voice cracking with urgency. "Another minute and they'll breach. You better move your ass."

Maddox ignored the comment, drawing closer to the intruders at a measured pace. The two corporati might know how to navigate the highfloor circles of power and influence, but they didn't know a thing about operating in VS. Even though his avatar was invisible to the intruders, concealed by a cloaking algorithm, if he came up on them too fast, their gear might detect his presence, and then they'd scatter like a flock of pigeons. But he couldn't move too slow, either. Every extra second he gave them was more time they had to get lucky and breach R&D.

Closer still. The fireflies darted back and forth next to the tall phosphorescent tower of brilliant white, the visual representation of R&D's digital self. Research and Development was one of two dozen similar building-like partitions, all clustered together like the downtown of some massive city, connected by an intricate latticework of pulsating data streams. Latour-Fisher Biotechnologies' datasphere—its digital skeleton and circulatory system, its brain, lungs, and heart—had become as familiar to Maddox over the past year as the lines of his own hand.

Closer. The spire of R&D now towered over him like a skyscraper, its ivory incandescence dominating his field of vision. The fireflies, still blissfully ignorant of his approach, bounced against R&D's outer wall. Trying and failing to breach the partition's protective barrier.

Two things would happen next. First, the sniffer would finish its trace and give up the trio's physical location, which he'd pass along to an emergency police feed, and the nearest on-duty cops would be dispatched to arrest the trio. And to make sure they didn't go anywhere, once Maddox was close enough, he'd hit all three with an envenomed algorithm, a program that would freeze their avatars in virtual space and paralyze their real-world meat sacks from wherever it was they were operating. Getting frozen was no fun, as they'd soon find out. They'd lose all motor control, going as stiff as day-old corpses, wide awake but helpless until the cops arrived and manually unplugged them by removing the trodebands around their heads. After that came handcuffs and a courtesy ride in a police hover, then fingerprinting and delousing, then formal charges in front of a judge. A chain of events leading inexorably to a long prison sentence.

Shit flowed downhill.

Maddox was almost close enough to unleash the algorithm. If the kids had been careful, they would have asked a standby to keep an eye on them while they were plugged in, someone who'd pull off their trodebands at the first sign of them being frozen. Though he knew such a precaution was unlikely. When he'd been a green datajacker, young and spirited and ignorant of his own vulnerability, he and his friends had made fun of suckers who used standbys, who needed a mommy or a daddy to watch over them. Things hadn't changed much since then, and these kids were probably doing the same dumb thing he'd done, operating without a safety net.

A chime tinkled in his ear—the sniffer completing its trace. He checked the map. The kids were in Queens, one of his old stomping grounds. He noted all three tags shared the same geo vector. Amateur hour, he thought, vaguely disappointed. They didn't even had the good sense to plug in from separate physical locations. They were making it easy for the cops.

Back in the conference room dickhead one spoke. "All three in the same place," he chirped, delighted. "Fish in a bloody barrel. Tag 'em."

Maddox hesitated. He hated this part of his job.

"Did you hear me?" the executive said, louder. "Tag those fuckers."

It's a good job, he told himself again. Don't fuck it up.

His hands gestured a command, and above each firefly a series of numbers appeared, their geographic location in longitude, latitude, and altitude. Maddox subvocalized another command, and the three geotags blinked red a few times, then went solid green as their locations were registered in the emergency police feed. A moment latera time estimate appeared, visualizing as a stopwatch shaped like a police badge.

"ETA's ninety seconds," Maddox said.

"That's more like it," dickhead one said, then slurped his latte. Maddox imagined the lid coming off, hot coffee spilling all over the man's crotch.

Ninety seconds. In less than two minutes, somewhere in Queens a door would be kicked in by a squad of local cops, and three pimple-faced kids with cobbled-together street gear and cheap trodebands around their heads would learn more than they ever wanted to about datajacking's downside.

Maddox stopped two grid clicks short of the quivering little fireflies, now the size of ping-pong balls. All three were still utterly unaware of his presence. Unsurprising, since Maddox had mastered data shielding and concealed approaches long before these kids had ever touched a set of trodes. He was thirty-one, and he could easily imagine the kids on the other end of those avatars being half his age or less. He'd started datajacking at fifteen, flirting with disaster at first just like these three. Plugging in with no standby and zero precautions, so eager to become a hotshot datajacker. Back before Rooney had taken him in and taught him how to plan a robbery like a professional. He wondered what Rooney would think of him if his old mentor could see him now.

"The hell you waiting for?" dickhead one sneered. "Freeze those cocksuckers."

He had to get on with it. Subvocalizing a command, he released the algorithm. Appropriately, its appearance mimicked a trio of snakes, deep violet in color, winding a menacing path through virtual space toward the intruders. Two wrapped themselves around their targets immediately, bringing the avatars' movements to an abrupt stop. The fireflies hung frozen in space, totally immobilized. The third snake darted back and forth as if confused, searching for a target that was no longer there.

No…way…

The third firefly was inside R&D, just beyond the partition's wall. The impossible had happened: a critical breach. And it had happened right under Maddox's nose. With executives watching him.

No vocabulary he had on quick recall could express the shock and dread that shot through him. *Oh, fuck!* and *oh shit!* fell far short. *Oh my God!* was nowhere in the neighborhood. He'd once heard a little Asian girl scream *shitfuck* over and over after burning her finger on a food stand's hotplate. After a stupefied moment, shitfuck was the word that sprang forth.

Shitfuck, shitfuck, shitfuck!

Maddox bit the inside of his cheek to keep himself from saying it out loud. "Cops get there yet?" he asked the executives, neither of whom had yet noticed the disaster.

A pause as they checked the police feed. Dickhead two answered. "Three more flights of stairs, they're saying. Twenty seconds, maybe fifteen."

No elevator, naturally. It just had to be a walk-up, didn't it? Twenty seconds was an eternity. If you knew what you were doing, you only needed five to jack a sizable chunk of R&D's intellectual property.

"Wait? What the hell just happened in there?" dickhead one said. "Where's the third one?"

Already scrambling into an improvised Plan B, Maddox didn't answer.

"Jesus," dickhead two whined, as if he'd just spilled something on his shirt. "He breached R&D."

Yes, Maddox agreed silently, he did. The one who wasn't totally clueless somehow pulled it off. And the cops in Queens wouldn't get there soon enough. The kid could scoop up a nice chunk of company IP and shoot it up to an orbital data haven, where an AI would gladly arbitrage it and place the proceeds in an untraceable account. And that would be that. The kids would still get busted seconds later, of course, but by then Maddox's career in the corporate world would already be over.

Back in the conference room, his hands made urgent gestures. Sharp movements he hoped the directors wouldn't recognize. In virtual space, white lines drew themselves in front of him, mirroring the paths of his flesh-and-bone fingertips.

"What are you executing in there?" dickhead one demanded. "That doesn't look proprietary."

"It's not," the other one cut in angrily. "Looks like street tech."

"Oh, no, you don't," dickhead one warned, his voice rising. "Don't even think about pulling up some unapproved app in there. You're liable to crash the whole system."

Maddox finished calling up the program, a slammer executable. He'd modded it himself in his spare time, recoding the defaults and removing the fail-safes, but he hadn't tested it yet. It was a less-than-ideal moment for a trial run, admittedly, but it was the only tool he had on hand that might work.

"Shut that thing down, NOW!" A finger poked

him in the back, hard. Maddox felt his own hand slap it away.

"If you want to come in here and help," he snapped, "be my guest. Otherwise, shut the fuck up and let me do my job."

He pictured the directors back in the conference room staring at him, having their own shitfuck moment. Two sets of corporati eyes wide with surprise, two executive mouths hanging open. No one ever talked to them like that. Certainly not some entry-level analyst. But Maddox was out of time, and he needed them off his back so he could concentrate. If the kid managed to jack company IP, a few harsh words to some higher-ups would be the least of his worries.

Deep…breaths. He concentrated, letting his awareness slip further into VS. The meat-and-bone machine of his body faded away completely, as did the panicked voices of the directors, now shouting at him to stop. His consciousness untethered, a euphoria settled over him, a warm feeling of invulnerability, of limitless capability, a jolt far better than any drug.

The slammer floated in virtual space, between him and the partition's outer wall, pulsing alternately red and blue, its bulbous head and trailing tentacles like some kind of ethereal jellyfish. Moving forward, Maddox projected himself onto the program, gasping as he adjusted to his new way of seeing. The exterior of the R&D partition was no longer solid like a building's exterior. It was opaque like frosted glass, and he could see the restless bustle of data coursing throughout its interior. Multicolored shapes of all sizes, zipping up and down and sideways. Uncountable bytes of information flowing through the structure like some circulatory system on hyperspeed overdrive.

And one virtual meter away from him, barely inside, he spied the third firefly.

The kid would be overwhelmed at first, Maddox knew. When you landed inside a data structure of this size and density, it felt like stepping out of a calm, quiet house into a raging thunderstorm. For a newbie, it would feel more like a tornado. The kid would need a few moments to get his bearings.

Still, he had to move quickly. He had no time for stealth, no time to shut down R&D's automated countermeasures. A smash-and-grab was his only chance.

Lunging forward, he crashed through the outer wall, sending shards of blinding light flying through space. Intruder alarms filled his ears. The partition's countermeasures would be on top of him in milliseconds, freezing him the same way he'd frozen the two newbies. He had to get to the third kid before that happened. Extending his tentacled arms, he reached out for the firefly, missing it entirely. Now aware of Maddox's presence, the intruder's avatar shot upward and away, hitching a ride on a large cylindrical data stream. Maddox rushed after him, barely able to track the avatar, so small and insignificant in the dense chaos of pulsing lights. He bared down, closing the distance, shooting the slammer's appendages at the intruder. He'd nearly reached it when he felt his body shudder, a jolt of cold hitting him. The countermeasures had him, wrapping him in their frigid grasp. For an instant, he pictured Rooney shaking his head at him, a rueful smile stretched across his face.

Now or never, he could almost hear Roon say.

A second, more powerful shudder blurred Maddox's vision, and a painful freezing cold overwhelmed him. He summoned all his energy and thrust forward, reaching through the narrowing tunnel of his perception toward the little firefly. Grabbing it and, finally, immobilizing it.

*   *   *

Minutes later, dickhead one stared at him, fuming. "It could have easily gone the other way."

"Very easily," two echoed, his stare equally harsh. In the stale fluorescent light of the conference room, the acne scars covering the man's cheeks looked like a scattering of craters on a dead moon.

"But it didn't," Maddox replied, rubbing his temples, still woozy from the encounter. His trodeband lay on the tabletop, the rounded plastic attachments shiny with sweat. The skin of his forearms prickled with goose bumps. Aftereffects of the countermeasures.

He'd neutralized the third newbie before any IP had been stolen. But it hadn't exactly been a textbook operation, and it was the means, not the end, that had the directors furious with him.

Dickhead one stood up from his chair, buttoned his suit coat. "That street tech you opened up in there. Looks more like a virus than a legitimate program. Probably take the data architects a week to fix the hole you punched into R&D. And God knows what it corrupted."

"Sloppy," his companion added, also standing. "Sloppy as hell. You should have known better than that."

Right. *He* should have known better. It took no small effort for Maddox not to argue back, not to blurt out the ugly truth: that none of this was his fault.

The executives had known going in there was a risk of a critical breach. Not a large one—less than a fraction of a percent, Maddox guessed—but still, they knew damned well it was a possibility. Maybe that was why they were so pissed. They'd been looking for a diversion, a break from an otherwise monotonous day of meetings and calls, and instead they'd ended up having to deal with the unexpected mess of a breach. Executives hated few things more than unexpected messes.

The whole thing was supposed to have been a bit of harmless spectator sport. The sport they'd heard about from their highfloor colleagues, probably over martinis in the executive lounge. What fun they could have when some clueless would-be infiltrators came along.

The sport in question was as straightforward as it was cruel. When aspiring data thieves like the still-frozen trio—typically kids with good gear and bad judgment—were detected by the datasphere's outermost monitoring apps, it was a dead giveaway the would-be datajackers were unskilled amateurs. It was something like a wannabe burglar scouting out a security fence with a pair of wire cutters in his hand…in broad daylight…right next to the security guard station. Zero threat level, in other words.

On such occasions, highfloor corporati like the two dickheads would often delay the capture of such bumbling crooks intentionally, the same way a cat might toy with a maimed rat before finally killing it. Though the execs never did the maiming and killing themselves, of course. Highfloor corporati didn't stoop to donning a trodeband and plugging into VS to nab datajackers. That was grunt work, far below their pay grade. Instead they'd call Blackburn Maddox, that security analyst they'd heard about who'd once been a datajacker himself, and summon him to a conference room where they'd watch him chase down the intruders, enjoying the spectacle of their corporate hound hunting down three helpless rabbits. A welcome bit of fun in an otherwise boring day of endless staff meetings and conference calls. And if by chance an intruder lucked out and managed to breach a critical partition, no big deal. Automated countermeasures would freeze his avatar before anything bad could happen.

That was how it was supposed to work, anyway, from the executive point of view, from the black-and-white perspective of the floors far above Maddox's head. The realities of virtual space, though, were far less cut-and-dry. Nothing was ever straightforward in VS. Beginners got lucky sometimes. Countermeasures could fail. Maddox had known this for the entirety of his datajacking career, and he was sure the executives knew it, too. Just like he was sure they'd never admit to as much, knowing that any such concession would imply their own guilt in this particular mess. In the remote possibility of a critical breach, it would be far easier—and from a career perspective, far more practical—to hang the blame, say, around the neck of a low-level analyst, who for some reason didn't freeze those little fireflies as quickly as he should have.

Maddox kept his eyes fixed on the table. There

was no point in arguing back. Even though nothing had ultimately been stolen. Even though he knew the executable he'd released was sterile, and the damage he'd caused was so minimal an intern could patch it up in a single afternoon. The executives were in no mood to hear any of that. All they'd wanted was to sit there with their coffees and enjoy the cat-and-mouse spectacle, and instead this ex-datajacker some idiot recruiter had been stupid enough to hire had dropped a problem into their laps. A problem they could easily explain away, sure, but a problem nonetheless. Then he'd busted out some street tech in their datasphere and been insubordinate on top of it.

To put it mildly, the two dickheads were not happy at the moment, and they glowered over Maddox like furious angels, determined to make this lowly mortal pay for his sins.

The holo display, floating a half meter above the conference table, blinked over to a communication feed. A cop in rhino armor stood in the foreground, his helmet removed to reveal a pudgy, sweaty face. Behind him was an arrest scene: three teenage boys on their knees, staring dumbly at the floor, hands manacled behind their backs. A pair of rhino cops wielding stubby automatic rifles stood over them, their bulky armor a comically massive contrast to the cramped, tiny apartment. A dingy bedsheet hung as a window cover, and a mess of datajacking gear lay strewn about. Trodes and generic decks and holo projectors littered the floor—most of it off-the-shelf stuff—along with a scattering of pizza boxes and Chinese takeout containers.

"All three targets secured, sir," the cop huffed, still breathing heavy from the upstairs sprint. "I was about to call it in."

The directors exchanged glances. "Let's not do that quite yet, Officer," dickhead one said. "If you don't mind, we'd like to…have a chat…with these intruders before you take them in."

"Understood," the cop answered, his tone and expression unchanged, as if he'd been expecting this exact request, which of course he had. Because this was the final portion of the wicked little game, the part corporati always took great pleasure in. And after all this trouble, the two dickheads certainly weren't going to let a minor breach get in the way of this, the best part of the game.

The cop turned and nodded to his companions, who nodded knowingly back. Then they reached to their belts, removed their shocksticks, and waited for the executives' instructions.

The torture that followed, micromanaged by the two executives, lasted well over an hour.

2
CAGED CRICKET

Maddox didn't call a ground car to take him home, opting instead to walk the fifteen-block haul from the company's HQ to his apartment. A spatter of rain fell, leaving a speckle of drops on his overcoat's collar and shoulders. He stepped off the curb and crossed Canal Street, heading uptown, losing himself in the chaotic embrace of the City.

It was night, a couple hours past sunset, a fact knowable only by the time readout superimposed on the lower corner of his specs. At street level, on the crowded floor of the City's deep, ever-bustling canyons, the cycles of day and night had long since lost any significance. The unnoticed sky was a hazy smudge far overhead, a narrow strip of overcast gray between the colossal structures of the City. In the wealthier sections, atmospheric domes had usurped the sky, glowing a cheery blue during daylight hours, with billowy marshmallow clouds and a brilliant simulated sun mirroring the real one's daily east-to-west journey.

He ran a hand through his hair, fingers coming

away wet. Before signing on at the company, he'd sported a shaved head, and the City's frequent drizzle always felt like a cool, refreshing spray against his bare scalp. But a skin dome was too street for Latour-Fisher Biotech's elegant hallways and offices, so these days he sported the stylish cut of the moment, his brown hair cropped close on the sides and longer on top. In the rain it felt like a wet mop lying on top of his head.

Images from the torture session replayed in a constant churn, a movie in his head he couldn't switch off. The executives had refilled their coffees and settled in, chuckling at the boys' seizure-like contortions and vomiting. They singled out the one who'd breached R&D for special attention. A ginger kid, pale and freckled with a tangled mess of curly red hair. He got the worst of it, the cops drawing out his suffering until the kid finally shit himself. After five long minutes Maddox got up and walked out, ignoring the director, who shot him a stink-eyed look and asked him where the hell did he think he was going.

Now he walked the streets, the City's teeming throb of bodies, its light-and-noise show enveloping him, welcoming him back as it always did, into its lively, unsleeping bosom of endless distraction. Ground cars crept through clogged streets, shuttling passengers uptown and downtown. Walkways overflowed with pedestrian traffic. Ads scrolled across the lower third of his lenses, targeting his profile—early thirties, male, Anglo, well-dressed, unaccompanied—with pitches for goods and services someone like him might be inclined to purchase on a whim at this hour in this part of the City.

"Jizz on my face, salaryman?" A neon blue woman, naked except for a pair of pink high heels, blew him a kiss from a doorway of arched brickstone. Letters appeared on the wall above her, superimposing themselves in the same color as the woman's skin. VIRTUAL FUN OR IN THE FLESH. WHATEVER YOU WANT, HOWEVER YOU WANT IT.

"Come in out of the rain." She crooked a provocative finger at him, her outstretched hand flickering as the drizzle passed through the holo, ruining the illusion. He walked on, and more offers came as he entered and exited the short-range broadcast cones emitted from storefronts and mobile vendors. Urgent whispers in his ear, transmitted through his spec's temple arm. Wares and narcotics one block. Ramen and kimchi the next. In the near distance, enormous ads flashed across building facades. A twenty-story Belgian Honey beer can popped open, froth spraying ten stories higher. A succession of postcard shots from an orbital resort appeared and faded. Impossibly beautiful men and women, naked and tanned, lying on artificial beaches, snorkeling in low-g lagoons. Live your dream today. Interest-free financing.

"Body mods, my friend? Half off retail." Maddox ignored the heavily accented Eastern Euro voice. His specs, a midrange pair of Venturellis, blocked most pop-up advertisements, but the street barkers' broadcasts still mostly managed to get through. He'd almost bought a higher-end pair, the kind that filtered out everything except the brands you preapproved, but then reconsidered when he saw the price.

Continuing uptown, he removed his specs and put

them away into a jacket pocket. He knew the way home. He didn't need a glowing path superimposed over the sidewalk to lead him to his building. Didn't need to see star ratings floating above taco stands. He didn't need to make any calls. Didn't want to receive any.

Did he still have a job? He didn't know. Were those kids in jail yet? He didn't know that, either.

They'd been dumb, those kids. Trying to jack a major corporation with no prep, no standbys. They had it coming. They were bound to get busted sooner or later. Whether it was by his hand or by some automated countermeasure or some watchdog AI, it was only a matter of time.

Keep telling yourself that, boyo. Maybe it'll help.

Great. That was all he needed, Rooney's ghost giving him stick. The voice of his old mentor asserted itself at unpredictable times, often telling Maddox what he least wanted to hear.

I did what I had to, Roon, he replied inwardly.

I know you did, but it still don't feel right, does it?

He wandered through thick knots of pedestrians, the City's ambient thrum in his ears. A police siren wailed a few streets over. Beat cops in bulky rhino armor, rifles in hand, appeared every few blocks, their faces hidden by darkened helmet visors. High overhead, hover taxis and limos, their distinctive high-pitched whine barely audible beyond the ground-level din, ferried the wealthy from building to building like bees floating among enormous hives. At street level, ground cars, a less expensive but far slower means of transportation, crept by at a glacial pace. For most of the City's residents, though, neither ground cars nor hovers were anywhere near affordable on their dole-based subsistence income. The ancient subway system, as it had for nearly three centuries, provided transportation for the largest, and poorest, portion of the City's populace. Subway exits disgorged hundreds at regular intervals from its underground tunnels.

Passersby noticed him, casting discreet, wary glances at the nakedfaced stranger. To be unspectacled in the City wasn't unheard of, but it was unusual, and somewhat conspicuous. The vibe he threw off was that of someone who wanted to be left alone. The street seemed to sense this, and recognizing it, gave him what he wanted. He moved through the crowded, bustling walkways, unmolested.

Elizabeth Street Garden appeared on his left, a tiny oasis of greenery wedged between slate-gray megastructures. Lining the sidewalks near the garden's entrance, pet vendors minded stacks of box-shaped cages. As Maddox approached, a cacophony of tweets and squawks rose above all other noises. Dozens of parakeets, parrots, and canaries shrieked and fluttered about inside cramped coops of wired metal.

"Modeados cien por ciento libre de enfermedades. Perfecto para los niños," a short, stubby-limbed vendor boomed. Modded one hundred percent disease-free, perfect for children. He repeated the phrase in Mandarin and Korean and Hindi, then after a short pause to let a fresh batch of potential customers come within earshot, he went back to Spanish and started the cycle again.

Wrinkling his nose at the smell, Maddox slid past the birdcages, stepping around fresh deposits of bird shit on the sidewalk, making his way to the end of the row, where the enclosures were much smaller. Atop an improvised table of plastic crates sat a collection of miniature cages constructed of bamboo. Delicate structures with bars the same color and thickness of uncooked spaghetti noodles. They housed a variety of crickets, spiders, grasshoppers, and other small insects.

Yoshi the bug man spotted him, flashing him a toothless grin as he pushed his wire-rimmed specs up his nose with a forefinger. He disappeared for a moment behind the crates, appearing again with a big smile and holding a lantern-shaped cage. Inside was a black-and-brown insect the size of Maddox's palm with thick, hairy legs and a segmented shell.

The bug man looked around furtively, then leaned forward and kept his voice low. "Hissing cockroach," he said, holding the tiny cage close to his body, as if it were a treasure too valuable to be revealed on a street corner. "From Madagascar. Very rare. For you I make special price."

"No, thanks," Maddox said, mildly amused he'd been tagged an easy mark by the little man. "Just need some cricket food."

"Very special price," the man persisted, lifting the cage and swaying it slightly, trying to entice his customer. "This last one. You come back tomorrow, all gone."

"Just the cricket food," Maddox replied, this time with a firmness the man couldn't mistake. Deflated, the bug man set the cage down and rummaged around behind the crates.

Next to Maddox, a child holding his mother's hand gawked at the collection of insects. "Mami, look, they're all in jail."

His mother chuckled. "What do you think they did to get in trouble, nene?"

"I don't know," the boy said. He thrust out his lower lip. "I feel sad for them, all locked up."

The bug man popped back up from behind the crates and grinned, shaking his head at the boy. "No, little sir. They *happy* in they houses. Very happy."

The boy looked skeptical. "Happy?"

"Yes! They get best food. Taken care of. No have to worry get eat by cat or bird or get step on by shoe."

The boy tilted his head, pondering the cages, seeming to reconsider his opinion.

Waving a crooked finger back and forth, the bug man said, "No jail, little sir. These no jails." He spread his hands wide, grinning. "Best home for them, all these pretty cages. No place better."

*   *   *

Maddox sat on his tenth-floor balcony, a narrow concrete rectangle jutting out from his apartment, barely large enough for him, a chair, and the smallest side table the local furniture store had in stock. He rolled a cigarette, yellow rice paper crinkling around fresh pinches of Balkan Sobranie he'd picked up earlier at the first-floor tobacco shop. He lit it, the tip glowing bright orange as he inhaled, the soothing smoke drawn into his lungs, then blown out again into the cool night air.

He flicked ash into a plastic Sapporo-branded ashtray he'd pocketed from a bar, recalling how the small act of thievery gave him a disproportionate pleasure. A tiny bit of lawlessness in an otherwise straight existence. Atop the small circle of the tabletop sat a tiny bamboo cage. A perfect cube not much larger than the ashtray next to it, the cage had a roof of thin, delicate wood—he wasn't sure what kind—with intricate carvings of flowers and leaves and gently curving, upturned pagoda-style corners. Maddox watched the box and the cricket inside, both purchased from Yoshi the bug man the week before. The cage was the priciest item at the stall, which was no doubt why the bug man had tried to sell him some high-end hissing cockroach earlier this night. If the silly white salaryman had picked up his most expensive item before, why not again?

The cricket inside chirped a soft rhythmic song, its mottled black-and-brown body visible only in glimpses in the moving shadows thrown off by the City's ceaseless animation of building-front ads and holos. From his balcony, the sound of the street was a steady, indistinct churn, like the murmur of a crowd, interspersed with the occasional siren's wail and, more frequently, the sudden, impatient choruses of ground car horns. Maddox pinched off a portion of the gelatinous feed he'd picked up earlier from the bug man. The cricketsong stopped as the creature approached the pea-sized meal, pausing a moment as if considering the offering, then it thrust its head onto the food and began its late dinner.

He smoked and gazed at the tiny caged creature. Would he have a job tomorrow? Did he have one now? Maybe the dickheads would let him off the hook. It had been a minor breach, after all, and nothing had been stolen. Still, the pair didn't strike him as the no harm, no foul types.

So if it was over, it was over. He'd never expected to end up in a salaryman's life. Never imagined himself lasting a day in a legit job at a legit company, much less a year. The fact that any of it had happened in the first place was something of a minor miracle.

He'd been hired thirteen months earlier, an unlikely candidate targeted by an ambitious recruiter looking "to fill knowledge gaps" in the company's data security division. *Filling knowledge gaps* had been corporate speak, an innocuous way of saying the company wanted to stock its talent pool with underground datajacking skills. Prior to his own recruitment, Maddox had heard of that sort of thing happening from time to time, legit companies hiring datajackers. Who better, after all, to sniff out a datasphere's security gaps and weaknesses than someone who'd made a living doing exactly that? The best among Maddox's former peers, however, whose illicit incomes far outsized a salaryman's pay, usually rebuffed any feelers from the legit world. Pay cuts weren't popular among the datajacking elite, first of all. And second, datajackers were born thieves, most of them proudly, even arrogantly so. The humdrum, straight-and-narrow life of a salaryman couldn't compare to the criminal glory of a top datajacker's existence.

Maddox knew that life, having once been among the elite of his profession, until a single disastrous gig had changed everything, taking the life of Logan Rooney, his longtime mentor, and poisoning his reputation among his fellow datajackers and those who hired them. After his fall from grace, he'd wandered the City in a months-long aimless funk. When the last of his cash had all but run out, fate had intervened in the form of the Latour-Fisher recruiter, a woman named Montoya, who'd managed to track him down. A blur of interviews and assessment tests had followed, culminating days later in one of the greatest shocks of Maddox's life: a job offer. He accepted, figuring what the hell, what did he have to lose, and it wasn't like people were beating down his door anyway. He entered the legitimate world at thirty, having spent half his life on the other side of legality, datajacking organizations not unlike the one that had just put him on its payroll. Strange times, indeed.

In the year since, he'd played it straight, following the rules, doing what he was told, keeping his nose clean and his head down. The straight life had taken some getting used to. Paying bills, opening bank accounts, signing a condo rental contract. The little things non-criminals breezed through without a second thought were to him unfamiliar, slightly jarring experiences.

As the square peg in a workplace full of round holes, he hadn't fit in at Latour-Fisher from the start. His colleagues didn't like him, especially the corporati, the wealthy, highly placed execs like the two dickheads. To them Maddox was street scum. No academic pedigree. No friends in high places. He was a mistake, a hire that never should have happened. The beneficiary of an ill-conceived initiative cooked up by some overzealous recruiter. He might have dressed like any other data security analyst, shared their same hairstylist, but the company men and women didn't consider him one of their kind. His peers and higher-ups, even the unpaid interns a decade younger than him, rarely missed an opportunity to remind him of his outsider roots.

He blew smoke out from the balcony as the cricket chirped its song. Somewhere high above, the high-pitched drone of hover engines rose and fell.

Still, even with all its downsides and snubs and oddness, he couldn't deny the life had grown on him. Sure, there was no thrill in it. It was a calm lagoon of an existence compared to the treacherous, raging river he'd navigated most of his life. But that was part of its appeal: the stillness, the quiet, the freedom from worry. Most of his old crowd would have laughed at that, ridiculed him for being a low-rent sellout, a dutiful little cog in a big machine. But screw them. A little cog never had to lie awake at night, worrying about the cops breaking down its door. It never had to sweat when its next payday would come. Never had to picture itself doing time at Rikers Island. A little cog had safety and security, and those were no small things in a brutal, merciless world.

Yes, even with all its downsides, the life had grown on him. He was used to it now.

And he didn't want to lose it.

The soft tone of an incoming call. He turned and spied his specs, flashing green on the coffee table inside the condo. He blinked. It was well past midnight. Crushing out his cigarette, he picked up the cricket cage and went inside.

"Maddox," he answered, donning his specs, hoping the call was a wrong number.

It wasn't.

3
DRINKS IN THE CHATTER BUBBLE

It was Maddox's first trip to his building's rooftop hover platform, and when he stepped through the sliding doors into the glass enclosure, a twinge of disorientation poked at his insides. It was less acrophobia than the unfamiliar vista at this lofty altitude. He hadn't been up this high in a long time. When was the last time he'd been above a hundred? He searched his memory, recalling an almost-forgotten adventure from childhood, courtesy of a maintenance crew's misplaced security card. He'd stolen aboard service elevators, dodging doorguard bots and sneaking past surveillance cams, eventually reaching floor 105 before he was finally caught.

Beyond the glass vestibule, the City was calm and quiet, even peaceful, the constant thrum of the street far below and unheard. The rain had stopped, leaving a wet sheen over everything. There were no flashing ads and massive holos this high up. That was how you knew you were in the rich level of town. The wealthy valued peace and quiet. Only the infrequent whine of a passing hover broke the silence. Yellow headlights appearing in the foggy distance, the turbofan motors crescendoing as the vehicle approached and then whizzed past, red taillights disappearing a moment later.

He waited for his ride, still mulling over the call he'd received minutes earlier, still struggling to believe that he'd really received it. The personal AI of an executive vice president, one Jonathan Hahn-Parker, had called him, summoning him to a meeting. At first Maddox had thought it was a scam call or even a joke, but when he'd checked the connection, he'd noted the call had come in using the company's tightest encryption, the kind reserved only for executive communications. He'd suddenly felt as if the hand of some god had reached down from the clouds and thumped him on the forehead.

The matter couldn't wait until morning, the machine's voice had said, then asked him politely to make his way to the hover platform, where a company car would pick him up in ten minutes. The entity had disconnected before Maddox could ask what the meeting was about.

Of course it had to be about the attempted datajacking earlier in the day. Had he screwed up in some way he wasn't aware of? Had his modded executable damaged something valuable? Corrupted company IP, God forbid? For an EVP to summon him at this hour, it had to be something pretty heavy.

He swallowed hard when the hover limo appeared out of the fog. Long, sleek, and bearing the Latour-Fisher Biotech logo, the obsidian-black vehicle came to a floating stop next to the building. Its six engine fans whined, the housings swiveling in minute, barely noticeable adjustments as it neared and then made contact with the platform. Locking into place with the telltale hiss-clank of a solid connection, the hover's door slid open and the vestibule's boarding bridge extended.

Inside, the hover was empty. Maddox climbed into the back, sinking into lush, cool leather he was too anxious to fully appreciate. The limo detached itself from the building and slid into the transit lane. Gentle acceleration pushed him back into the seat, and outside the rain started up again. Drops streaked sideways across the glass as the hover increased speed. He tried to relax as he watched the buildingscape pass by. He'd been in hover taxis a handful of times, but never a limo. And never this high up. Without the constant neon assault of flashing ads and holos, it was easier to see the shape of the buildings, the almost organic connectedness of the City's infrastructure. He recalled what Rooney had told him about the evolution of the City's architecture. How most structures in the City used to be standalones. Rooney had shared with him holos of the City from long ago. The image reminded Maddox of a pincushion with the buildings as freestanding needles. At some point, Rooney told him, the buildings had begun to grow into one another. Concrete embedded with cheap, disposable nanobots had been the innovation making the connections possible. No engineers or constructions crews needed. Just tell the bots to make a walkway connecting building A to building B, then sit back and watch them do their thing. And so the buildings slowly began to join together, connecting themselves like adjacent beehives growing together to form massive superhives. That was why they called them hiverises, Rooney said, the daisy-chained megastructures housing hundreds of thousands, even millions, of residents. Each one was a universe unto itself, a self-contained kingdom with its own customs and languages and food and styles of dress.

The rain abruptly stopped. Lost in thought, Maddox hadn't realized the hover had passed under a dome. He looked up through the limo's transparent roof, dotted with moisture. A star-filled sky and a crescent moon, too perfect to be true. Thin wisps of clouds drifted by, smoky and pale white in the reflected moonlight. A beautiful illusion animating the dome's underside, one he rarely saw since he almost never came to the domed sections of the City. The sky from his lowfloor world was a perpetual overcast gray, not that he looked up at it much. Two minutes later, he was still staring upward when the limo hiss-locked onto its destination platform.

The limo's door lifted open. He paused before getting out, took a gathering breath, then laughed inwardly at himself for bothering. There was no preparing for whatever was waiting for him. There was only getting it over with.

Exiting the limo, he was met by a woman. Fair-skinned and nearly his height, she wore a dark pantsuit and low-heeled Pradas. Dyed a light shade of slate, her hair was cut short on the sides, and on top a thick mane fell to one side, falling just below her jawline. She held herself more like a bodyguard than an executive, and Maddox pictured a strong, muscled frame beneath the business attire. She wore no specs.

"Mr. Maddox, welcome," she said, voice flat, her naked face expressionless. "I'm Beatrice. This way, please." She gestured, then stepped aside, and as

Maddox passed, a glint from the woman's eyes caught his attention. Her irises flickered slightly. A small thing, noticeable only from close up. He'd seen eye implants before, a few times, but they were rare, even among the wealthy.

She lifted an eyebrow. "What's the matter? Never seen any before?"

He broke eye contact and said, "Sorry. Didn't mean to stare."

They walked on. She was company security, he figured, or maybe Hahn-Parker's personal detail. He wondered what other mods she might have, hidden beneath her designer threads. The modded, especially security types, rarely stopped at a single enhancement.

They entered a hallway with a polished white marble floor and oil paintings decorating the walls. "What building is this?" he asked. With his gaze fixed on the dome's night sky, he'd missed exactly where the limo had dropped him off. Somewhere in Central Park West, he guessed, judging by the duration of his ride, the dome's presence, and the address's upscale first impression.

"Sembacher-Chan Tower 3," she answered.

He'd guessed right. SC's Tower 3 was one of Central Park West's most luxurious standalones, a mixed residential and commercial highrise housing the City's wealthiest businesses and private citizens. He was keenly aware how out of place he was, how rarefied the air he was breathing. A square foot of the real estate here was worth more than his entire condo.

The readout on his specs said one ten in the morning. Roughly half an hour had passed since Hahn-Parker's office had called. Maddox had never met the man, but he'd heard the name plenty. An executive vice president, Hahn-Parker sat on Latour-Fisher Biotech's board of directors with five others, four men and women and the company's AI. Aside from those few facts, he knew nothing about the man, but those facts were more than enough. As a Latour-Fisher board member, Hahn-Parker would be among the wealthiest, most powerful movers in the City.

The mystery of his summons still dogged him. Why would a topfloor corporati want to see him? If something had gone terribly wrong with the attempted datajacking, surely someone much lower down the food chain would have contacted him. None of this made sense.

They exited the hallway into the forty-ninth-floor atrium, the enormous open space that was the building's signature architectural feature. The cavernous expanse enclosed a country estate, or what Maddox thought of as a country estate. He'd only seen such things on entertainment holos. Perfectly manicured grass, pink granite walkways bordered by large leafy plants in chest-high ceramic pots, thick copses of trees with lush canopies reaching ten meters high. Set to an approximation of sunset, the lighting control cast a golden glow upon everything. He resisted the impulse to curse in amazement. The cost to build all this, to maintain it, had to be staggering. Rarefied air, indeed. The woman named Beatrice headed for the walkway. Maddox followed.

At the center of the grounds was Chateau Montmartre, a stone-by-stone replica of the original restaurant located in the Côte d'Azur. A postcard image of a quaint, rural cottage nestled in the foothills of the French countryside. A steady stream of the

City's elite—highfloor corporati, fashion models, movie actors, politicians—could be seen daily coming and going, but at this hour there was only Maddox and the woman and the sound of their footfalls echoing on the pathway.

She led him through the front door and across an empty, darkened dining room. Wide canvasses of impressionist landscapes adorned the walls. Large, ornate wooden chairs were neatly placed around tables in perfect geometry. They turned a corner and went through another door, where they found Jonathan Hahn-Parker alone in a private dining room, seated at a table covered with white linen. A small chandelier hung overhead, its lights dimmed. A small, squat candle burned at the table's center, and beside it, a crystal glass half-filled with an amber liquid Maddox guessed was an expensive scotch. Across from the executive, a second glass sat empty.

The man stood, smiled warmly, and extended his hand. "Jonathan Hahn-Parker, a pleasure." Fiftyish and trim with boyishly thick hair gone mostly gray, he gave off an air of quiet confidence. He wore a three-piece charcoal-gray business suit with a perfectly knotted tie of turquoise blue.

"Blackburn Maddox." They shook hands. Hahn-Parker removed his specs, a custom pair of Kwan Nouveaus, and gave them to the woman.

"Please, have a seat." Hahn-Parker gestured to the empty chair across from him.

"Your specs, please," the woman said.

Maddox nodded, removing his Venturellis and handing them to the woman. Relinquishing specs—a gesture Maddox hadn't expected—meant their meeting wouldn't be captured and archived by the lenses' automated archiving. A nakedfaced conversation implied the highest level of confidentiality. Given the circumstances, Maddox wasn't sure if this meant he was in less hot water or more.

"Drink?" Hahn-Parker offered, nodding to the empty glass.

"I'm fine, thanks," Maddox said, sitting down.

The woman placed a flat, round object on the table that looked like a metallic coaster. The executive pressed his thumb to it, and a green light appeared around the outer edge. Backing away from the table a couple meters, the woman touched a forefinger to her ear, apparently to a small earpiece Maddox hadn't spotted.

"All good," she said. "Solid wall."

Hahn-Parker nodded at her.

The woman left, closing the door behind her. Maddox stared at the coaster thing and blinked. "Is that a chatter bubble?"

"It is."

"I didn't think they made them that small." The ones Maddox had seen were the size of a small table lamp, and outrageously expensive. He couldn't imagine how much this one cost.

"I think the manufacturer only made six or seven." Hahn-Parker sipped his drink.

So, their conversation was going to be nakedfaced *and* take place inside a chatter bubble, an invisible spherical distortion field that not only garbled their speech to anyone listening from outside its two-meter radius, but also blocked outside parties from monitoring or capturing whatever was said inside. If you wanted zero chance of anything you said being understood or overheard, you said it inside the expensive privacy of a chatter bubble.

"Maybe I will have a drink," Maddox said.

The executive grinned. "Good man." Hahn-Parker reached down beside him and lifted up a bottle from the floor. He filled the empty glass in front of Maddox, refilled his own. "My apologies for the hour. I do thank you for coming on such short notice."

They drank. The scotch was insanely good, smoky and rich and full in his mouth, then luxuriously warm down his throat. He stole a second drink before returning the glass to the table.

The executive gazed at him. "So tell me how things are going for you at the company."

Small talk. At two in the morning. With an EVP. What exactly was going on? "Just fine."

"Just fine? That's all?" Hahn-Parker raised his eyebrows. "Yours is an enviable life, wouldn't you say? Do you know how many would trade places with you in the blink of an eye, times being what they are? Don't you feel fortunate, Mr. Maddox, for the opportunity fate has afforded you?"

"When you put it that way, sure."

The executive nodded, watching Maddox like he was pondering something deeper, more meaningful than his simple question and its simpler reply.

"I've followed your progress, and I have to say I'm impressed." Hahn-Parker took another drink.

Followed his progress? Maddox didn't know what to make of that. The notion that an EVP even knew his name seemed inconceivable, but following his progress? The idea bordered on the absurd. Someone in Hahn-Parker's position negotiated multibillion-dollar deals before breakfast, they didn't bother with the goings-on near the ground floor. It was like a god taking an interest in a housefly.

"You've performed well over this last year." The executive rotated the glass slowly in his hand. "Yesterday's events notwithstanding."

A sinking feeling stabbed at Maddox's insides. "So you know about that."

Hahn-Parker nodded. "I was told."

He was told. Wonderful. Maddox had a sudden urge to down the rest of his drink. "Sir, I know what I did wasn't exactly by the book, but—"

"But it worked."

"Yes."

"It did indeed, Mr. Maddox." Again the ponderous stare. "There's something to be said for a results-oriented mindset. Ends often justify the means, wouldn't you agree?"

"They can." Where was this conversation going? Was the man toying with him?

"Mr. Maddox. Blackburn, if I may, what occurred today with those juvenile delinquents doesn't concern me. If anything, it was a godsend, as it only reinforced my notion of how clever and resourceful you are."

All right, then, Maddox thought, now as baffled as he was anxious. If he wasn't in hot water for the barely avoided datajacking disaster, then what was he here about?

"I have an assignment for you," the executive explained. "A task I believe you're perfectly suited for."

Hahn-Parker paused, letting the words sink in. A task, Maddox repeated inwardly. A task I dragged you here at two in the morning to talk to you about, without specs, inside a chatter bubble.

He had it now. Only one explanation made sense.

"You want me to datajack somebody."

Hahn-Parker grinned. "As a matter of fact, I do."

4
GRAVY TRAIN

"There's nothing more despicable than a traitor." Hahn-Parker frowned as he stared into his glass, then took a long swallow.

The executive vice president sat across from Maddox, sharing the bottle of thirty-year-old single-malt scotch as he detailed a major breach of company security and how he wanted Maddox to help him resolve it. And as he did so, his plainspoken demeanor gave no indication he was discussing corporate espionage and felony-sized crimes. He might have been going over the details of a departmental expense budget for the lack of concern on his face and in his tone. Maybe the impenetrable wall of privacy put him at ease, Maddox thought. Or maybe the man had ice water in his veins instead of blood.

It took some minutes for Maddox to adjust to his strange new reality, to the thin air of these dizzying heights he found himself in. The scotch helped.

Two days prior, Hahn-Parker explained, a midlevel manager, angry over being passed up for a promotion, had stolen a small fortune's worth of company biotech IP, then sold the information to a black market data broker, a man named Novak. The name didn't ring any bells from Maddox's past, but then he didn't know everyone who dealt in stolen data.

"How'd you find out about it?" he asked.

"Loose lips sink ships," Hahn-Parker said. "Our man had one too many at a local tavern, it seems, and he boasted about his deed to some woman, hoping to impress her, I imagine. He went on about how he'd one-upped Latour-Fisher and made himself rich in the process. Fortunately for us, one of our directors was sitting nearby and overheard." The executive paused for a drink. "We brought the indiscreet fool in this morning. He made a full confession." Maddox wondered how many pops from a shockstick it had taken for the man to spill everything.

"Now the only loose end is our IP," the executive continued, "and that's where we can use your talents."

Maddox drank. "How do you know the broker still has it? He might have resold it already."

"Our turncoat swears he wasn't working with our competition on this, and that this Novak person purchased the data with the intention to shop it around. If that's the case, it's reasonable to assume the broker is still in possession of our IP."

Maddox nodded. "If that's true, he'll hang on to it for about a week," he said, "a week and a half at most." Back in the day he and Rooney had worked with brokers dozens of times, shopping chunks of stolen data. It never took less than a week to get bids back from all the major buyers.

"Then we must get to work quickly," Hahn-Parker said. "We'd like our IP retrieved as soon as possible."

"Retrieved?"

"Yes."

Maddox took a longer drink this time. "What about your backups?"

The executive shook his head. "Unfortunately, there are none. This particular project manager was overly protective of his work. One might even say paranoid. He stored portions of his research on his own private, portable archive, unbeknown to the company, of course. This portable archive, and the company IP it contained, were handed over to the broker in person, traded for two suitcases of cash. We could find no trace of any the archive's contents or any copies inside the company."

Maddox chewed on this. It was far from the first time he'd heard of such a scam: a malcontent employee secretly hoarding company secrets or sensitive data until they had a stash valuable enough to sell for a pile (or two suitcases) of money. Turncoats like these had provided Maddox and Rooney with easy work from time to time. They'd act as go-betweens for some straight-and-narrow corporati who'd managed to find them through the black market feeds. While they weren't in the business of fencing stolen data—they were datajackers, not brokers, after all—for a handsome fee they were happy to connect some clueless suit with the right contact in the underworld. Good work if you could get it.

Maddox shifted in his chair. "Why not just call the cops or the feds? Have some rhinos storm this Novak's condo and get your IP back?"

The executive nodded. "A fellow board member suggested as much. But let me ask you, if you needed to recover high-value, irreplaceable IP, would you select the police as your first recourse?"

Maddox didn't consider himself the ideal person to answer this question. Where he came from, nobody ever called the cops. Still, he got the man's point. If this Novak was like most brokers Maddox had known, he already had the archive locked down tight, probably even booby-trapped with high-end countermeasures. Cops, even the federal ones, weren't exactly the savviest technologists around, and they were as likely to destroy the data as recover it intact. If the IP was as valuable as the executive was claiming, he wouldn't risk getting the cops involved unless he had no other choice.

"Has anyone reached out to this broker?" Maddox asked. "Try to buy it back from him?" It would be the easiest, least complicated solution to the problem.

The executive blinked. "That's plan B."

Which implied Maddox was plan A, though it wasn't clear how that made sense.

"But a payoff's easier," he pointed out. "And a lot less risky."

Hahn-Parker swirled his scotch. "Why don't you let me worry about the company's risk, yes?" Underneath the polite tone, Maddox sensed annoyance. The highfloor corporati didn't like being second-guessed. "I convinced the board to give you three days to recover the dataset containing our IP. If you aren't successful—or if you choose not to assist us—then I'm afraid we'll be forced to negotiate a settlement with this data broker."

For a long moment, neither man spoke. Overhead, the chandelier cast its low light over them. A fly buzzed around one of the candelabras. It reminded

Maddox of the newbie datajackers from earlier in the day.

"So," the executive said, downing the rest of his drink, "can I count on your help?"

Maddox didn't say anything. He didn't know what to say. Didn't know what to think. A part of him was still reeling, still coping with the impossible trajectory of the past few hours.

Staring at him, Hahn-Parker seemed to understand this. "I can appreciate how overwhelming this is for you. Take the next few hours to let all this sink in, and if I haven't heard back from you by tomorrow morning, I'll know your answer." He pressed his thumb to the chatter bubble control. Green changed to red. The EVP stood and pocketed the device.

"Good evening, Blackburn. And thanks again for coming." He shook Maddox's hand, then exited the room.

When the door closed behind the man, Maddox sat there for a moment in silence. Then he helped himself to a last generous portion of scotch. Liquid amber sloshed into the glass. He downed it in a single swallow.

What a day.

*   *   *

Think of all the things that can go wrong, boyo.
Rooney had preached this to Maddox back in the day, repeating it like a mantra, every time they prepped for a datajack. You can't cowboy it, his mentor warned. You can't break into some company with no plan, thinking you were the shit, or some untouchable hotshot. Cowboy jackers might get lucky

a time or two, but they never lasted more than a few runs. No, you had to think of everything that could go wrong, and even then there'd still be a dozen things you'd missed.

Since the portable archive was, by its very nature, cut off from any digital connection, Hahn-Parker's task would by necessity be an onsite job. Maddox hated onsite jobs. They were messy, clumsy affairs. You had to physically break into someone's office or home or whatever, like some junkie looking for jewelry to hock at a pawnshop. And no matter how much intel you gathered up beforehand, something always got missed. An overlooked doorguard bot. A nervous neighbor who called the cops at the slightest odd sound or unfamiliar face passing through the lobby. Maddox had done a handful of onsite jobs in his time. None of them had gone off without a hitch. And a couple had nearly gotten him busted.

Wired and unable to sleep, after the limo dropped him off at his building, he roamed the neighborhood with his hands in his pockets. The earlier drizzle had lessened to a mist, settling over everything as if a cloud had descended onto the floor of the City. Crowded walkways, flashing lights, the motley fried smells of food kiosks. The teeming clamor of the street, unabated even at this hour, flooded his senses, and he welcomed its familiar embrace. When everything else in the world went sideways, the street never changed, and there was comfort in that.

He lit a cigarette. An ad reminding him to refill his tobacco supply appeared on the lower portion of his specs, fading away a moment later as he exhaled smoke.

It wasn't larceny in the strictest sense, of course.

After all, it was the company's IP in the first place, so he wouldn't actually be stealing anything. He'd be recovering stolen goods. As soon as the thought struck him, he laughed inwardly at the half-assed rationalization. If he got busted, this technicality would hardly matter, since he'd have to rack up half a dozen felonies and datacrimes to reach the archive in the first place.

He smoked and walked on. Energy soda ads popped up on his lenses. Cartoon animals sang a pet food jingle as they chorus-lined up the side of a nearby building. Beyond the lenses, the street's neon kaleidoscope whirled around him, vying for his attention. Lost in thought, he saw nor heard any of it.

When he'd first started with the company, he'd suspected they might have hired him to perform tasks exactly like this one. Illegal datajacking jobs, in other words. It was his specialty, after all, the skill he brought to the table. His "value-add," as the marketers would say. In his former life he'd heard about megacorporations retaining their own in-house jacking talent, payrolled data thieves who'd opportunistically steal from competing firms when the need arose. The war for market share was fierce, and most companies viewed corporate espionage as a necessary evil.

But after months of employment at Latour-Fisher, he hadn't once met another person with his background or his particular skills, and the tasks he'd been given were no different than the ones his security analyst colleagues were assigned. Writing security scripts, patching weak spots in the company's datasphere, and so forth. Maddox had long since dismissed the notion of corporate datajackers as so much gossip. Until today happened.

He could say no, of course. Hahn-Parker had left that possibility open to him, though there seemed little doubt a refusal was tantamount to career suicide. You didn't say no to an EVP, no matter what the question was. But Hahn-Parker knew Maddox wouldn't say no, just like Maddox knew it himself. They both had known it from the moment he'd walked into that darkened room and sat down for drinks inside the chatter bubble. Whatever the highfloor corporati would ask of him, he was going to say yes.

Because he had skin in the game now.

The legit life, he had to admit, had grown on him. Over the past year, he'd become comfortable inside his corporate refuge, accustomed to his salaryman's life. Sure, there were the constant snubs and rude reminders of his outsider status, but those were minor inconveniences, soft punches he could take without flinching.

The company was an impenetrable cement bunker in a war zone. Inside its corridors, the brutal world he'd known as a child seemed like some distant memory. That one-room run-down with a leaky, rust-stained ceiling. A dented government-issue food fabber dispensing calorie allocations of tasteless, spongy breadcake. Weekly rhino cop raids, the heavy thud of armored footsteps in the hallway, flashes of gunfire under the door, his belly flat against the floor, hands clasped over his ears.

Latour-Fisher Biotech paid him well. Not hover limo well, but well enough to afford a decent rental in a good building, to dine in four-star restaurants (five-star on special occasions), to buy nice suits. It was steady money, too, not the feast or famine scramble of a datajacker's life. And he never had to worry about a cop busting through his door and shocksticking him.

His impoverished childhood, his data-thieving young adulthood. Both seemed a million miles away now, and a million miles away was where he wanted to keep them.

And he couldn't deny enjoying the stature that came with working at Latour-Fisher. The respect he didn't get at the workplace was more than offset by the envious awe of nearly everyone outside of it, when they learned the prestigious address where he worked Monday through Friday. Megacorporations like Latour-Fisher sat at the top of the food chain. Higher than cops, higher than city councils, higher than entire governments. They held immeasurable wealth and exercised all-but-unchecked power. And if you worked for the company, you were someone special, someone who was catered to. A one-percenter. Your association with an outfit like Latour-Fisher got you a better table at a restaurant, better service from a bank, preferential pricing almost everywhere. It got you laid, quite often.

Stamping out his cigarette, he spotted a seat opening up at a ramen stand. He shouldered his way through the crowd and slid onto the plastic stool. The stand's proprietor, a tiny man with a paper hat, nodded at him from behind a curtain of steam. Reaching for a pair of chopsticks, Maddox ordered a soyu bowl and a Kirin.

So he was going to datajack for the man now. What would Rooney say if he could see him? Would he laugh and call him a soulless sellout? Or would he

just stroke his beard and say nice move, boyo? Ride
that gravy train for as long as you can.

5
TAILING THE SALARYMAN

Beatrice saw nothing special about this Maddox person on first impression. But then most corporati, vain and shallow and absurdly status-conscious, didn't impress her. Still, he'd been summoned by one of the company's top suits, so she wouldn't put much stock in first impressions.

She followed him from a discreet two-block distance. On the jammed streets of his neighborhood, she might as well have been ten kilometers away. Even if he whirled around and looked in her exact direction, he'd never spot her in the churning pedestrian sea. From her perspective, though, he was easy to pick out, despite the crowd and the constant distractions of giant holo ads and street barkers. For floating above the salaryman's head, a downward-pointing cone followed him, a shape visible only to her. The company had given her the geo PIN for his specs, allowing her to tag him, and now he was as easy to follow as a child toting a giant red balloon.

For an undomed area, the neighborhood's street level wasn't half-bad. Passable food, fewer beggars and less general squalor than much of the rest of the City. The crowd was young, mostly tadpole corporati, twentysomething execs-in-training who earned decent salaries and walked with fast, purposeful strides. Always in a hurry, always talking fast. Assholes, for the most part.

She tailed the salaryman, her corporati disguise branded perfection, down to the Granville specs with untreated glass lenses. She didn't need a working set of specs, since her own eyes, a pair of artificial implants hardwired to her optic nerves, were far more advanced than even high-end military-grade specs. She'd purchased them from an off-grid Chinatown clinic that specialized in such things. They hadn't been cheap, but she'd found them to be worth every dollar she'd paid. Over the years she'd invested a small fortune in her eyes and a dozen other upgrades and genehacks, not a single one of them legal.

In her line of work, the unmodded were the unemployed.

She followed the salaryman as instructed, even though she found it a bit overkill, not to mention hopelessly antiquated. The executive could have tracked the salaryman on his own, or even had the cops keep an eye on him via streetcam feeds. Hell, he could have had one of the company's bumblebee drones follow Maddox, hovering over his head, totally unseen, recording every step the guy took. But no, he'd insisted on an off-the-radar tail. No drones, no cops, no official corporate resources. And if it looked like the salaryman was trying to skip town, heading for the train station or the airport, she was to call Hahn-Parker immediately. The EVP was the paying party, so she didn't question it. If he wanted her to tail the salaryman until morning the old-fashioned way, fine by her.

Still, it triggered a rumble of uncertainty in her, a sense of something not quite right about this gig. Something besides the fucked-up way she'd been recruited.

"Hey, baby, where'd you get those specs?"

A man to her left, matching her stride for stride, smiled at her stiffly. Before she could react, he leaned forcefully against her with his shoulder. Shoved off-balance, she stutter-stepped sideways, and then suddenly there was a second man, his hand locked around her upper arm, pulling her. In less than a second, she'd been jostled off the avenue and into a darkened narrow alleyway.

The two men were young, sloppily dressed, and had the feral, half-starved look of fighting dogs. Pharma freaks, she guessed, jonesing for a fix. They shoved her deeper into the alley, their backs to the avenue, blocking her from the view of passersby, none of whom stopped or even looked in her direction.

Beatrice looked the pair up and down, then rolled her eyes. "Boys, you really don't want to do this." Her voice was controlled and firm. A show of confidence might be all she needed to back them down. She didn't want to fight. A fight brought attention, and attention was something you didn't want when you were tailing someone.

Her lack of fear seemed to confuse them. The pair shot each other uncertain glances.

Beatrice stared them down. "You're going to let me walk past. All right?" She pulled a sheaf of hard currency from her jacket pocket. "You can have this.

All you have to do is let me by."

The shorter one rocked back and forth nervously on the balls of feet. The taller one rubbed the tips of his thumbs and forefingers together in quick, manic strokes. It was anybody's guess what they were on. Home-fabbed narco labs offered hundreds of flavors. They were everywhere these days, and about as easy to find as a taco stand.

She stepped forward, her hand extended with the cash. The shorter one turned sideways, giving her space. She slid by, handing over the notes. She'd almost exited the alley when a hand came down hard on her shoulder, yanking her backwards and off her feet.

She flailed and fell hard against the pavement. They stood over her, their bodies tense, hands balled into fists. She sat in a rainwater puddle, legs splayed out, her rear smarting where she'd landed.

"She's got jewelry, I bet," the shorter one said.

"And those specs. I bet those specs are worth a shitload."

She checked the state of her clothes. Her pants and the lower portion of her jacket were soaked with filthy water, probably ruined. Turning her face upward, she gave them an annoyed look.

"The specs are fake, you fucking amateurs." She gripped her jacket lapels. "But this...this is Versace." She stood up from the puddle and cracked the knuckles of her right hand. "Do you know how often a client buys me Versace?" The junkies sneered at her. "Almost never," she said.

The taller one rushed her and the world instantly went into slow motion. Surging adrenaline triggered designer neurochems, amping her senses, reflexes, and muscle strength. She caught him on the point of the chin with a punch he never saw coming. Her granitelike fist—the bones of her hands hardened by a series of nanotech treatments in Brazil—collided against his jaw, shattering it like a sheet of ice struck with a hammer. Her attacker dropped to the ground, a heap of arms and legs, the lower portion of his face grotesquely misshapen.

Beatrice stepped over the fallen junkie. The shorter one's eyes went large and white, his mouth hanging open in disbelief.

Beatrice cracked the knuckles of her left hand.

"Choices," she said calmly. "Life's a series of choices, kid. And the way I see it, right now you've got two." She motioned toward the ground. "One: you can try to avenge your buddy here." She wrinkled her nose, shook her head. "Personally, I wouldn't recommend it. Or two: you can turn around, run out of this alley, and save yourself a trip to the hospital."

He was gone before she'd finished the sentence. She brushed her hands against her rear, straightened her sleeves and jacket tails, and sighed. "Versace," she muttered at the unconscious man lying in a puddle.

Minutes later, she caught back up with her target. The salaryman had parked himself at a ramen stand, a plastic cup of beer in front of him. The seat next to him was open. She sat down just as the noodle man placed a steaming bowl in front of him.

He recognized her on a double take and set down his chopsticks. "You?"

"Me," she said.

He noticed her wet, damaged clothes. "What happened to you?"

"Slipped and fell." She lifted her chin at the noodle

man, then tilted her head toward the salaryman. "Same as he's having."

The salaryman furrowed his brow. "Wait a second. Were you following me?"

"Good ramen here?"

He blinked. "Best in the City."

"So you're on board, I take it?"

He nodded slowly. "How did you know?"

"This looked like a post-decision snack to me. And you didn't strike me as the stupid type who'd say no."

He straightened up. "What type do I strike you as?"

The noodle man placed her bowl and beer in front of her. "The type who's buying me an early breakfast." She grabbed a pair of chopsticks. "Don't mind, do you? I'm all out of cash."

"Sure," he muttered. "My pleasure."

She lowered her head to the bowl, slurped a mouthful of noodles. "Damn. Not bad."

The City teemed all around them, the noodle stand a tiny island in a flowing river of pedestrians.

"So what now?" the salaryman asked.

Beatrice slurped another mouthful, savoring the flavor. Maybe this salaryman was special and maybe he wasn't, but he did know his ramen.

"Now you grab a few hours' sleep," she replied. "Then we'll go meet your crew."

6
TARGET PRACTICE

After sunup, the mercenary woman Beatrice brought Maddox, bleary-eyed and sleep-deprived, to a section of the City near Pier 88. The place reminded him of the neighborhood he'd grown up in. It was that much of a shithole. Abandoned streets, silent as a graveyard. No pedestrians or ground cars. No food kiosks stood on corners. No holo women beckoned. No towering projected beer cans overlaid the crumbling facades of the dying buildings—only a chaos of faded graffiti tags. The separation of walkway and roadway was indistinguishable under a ragged carpet of throwaway plastics and sodden foamboard. The air was thick with moisture and the stink of rot. High above the low-rise structures stood the Twelfth Avenue Seawall, massive and towering, like some looming, disinterested god.

The taxi had dropped them off five blocks short of their requested destination, its automated voice apologizing, informing them it had reached the limit of its service area. Maddox grumbled as he climbed out, though he wasn't surprised. It was the kind of place automated taxis got disabled and stripped for parts in about two minutes. Dank, trashed-out seawall districts like Pier 88 were the City's pocket anarchies, thinly populated by squatters and junkies and narcofabbers. As he stepped onto the walkway, Maddox's specs kept flashing warnings about crime statistics and potential biohazards.

He blinked them away.

He wasn't sure how long he'd slept the night before, tossing and turning until he finally nodded off, dozing for what seemed like a handful of minutes before the mercenary woman's call had awakened him with a jolt, interrupting some weird dream about insects. Now she walked a step ahead of him, alert and taking in their surroundings. He stole a furtive glance at her eyes, the perfect irises a curiosity to the technician in him. He wondered what she saw with the implants, where she'd acquired them. Only the wealthiest could afford such enhancements, though even among the rich, specs were still the standard, the ubiquitous technology that had supplanted the cell phones and personal computing devices of a previous age. He'd once seen a news feature that attempted to explain the slower-than-expected adoption of tech that directly interfaced the optic nerve. The general reluctance to move from specs to ocular implants, a social scientist had claimed, was had less to do with its enormous expense than with the irreversible nature of the procedure, the huge leap of technological faith it required. Specs, after all, you could take on and off. If you got tired of one pair, you could toss them out and buy another. But once you upgraded to artificial eyes, that was it. There was no turning back. Very few, it seemed, were willing to take that irreversible step, to permanently connect their meat to the cybernetic.

The hired fist Beatrice, who clearly held no such reservations, scanned the block, clad in black jeans, matching cotton undershirt, and a chestnut-colored leather jacket.

"Next building on the right." She motioned to an old warehouse, a dilapidated box-shaped structure sitting beyond an open lot of tangled weeds. Twists of steel rebar poked out from the overgrowth, hinting at the remains of a concrete foundation, hidden like some long-forgotten corpse.

"You pick this location?" Maddox asked.

She nodded. "Seemed out of the way enough. Street cams around here were torn down years ago. Cops never bothered to replace them."

"So where'd you find this crew?" Maddox asked.

"I didn't," she said.

"Then who did?"

"Big boss man."

Maddox stopped. "An executive vice president handpicked a crew for a datajacking job?"

She shrugged. "I know. Doesn't smell right to me either."

"Did you ask him where he found them?"

"Of course I asked. He didn't want to give it up."

"So how'd he find *you*, then?"

She hesitated. "I came highly recommended."

He didn't bother pursuing it, sensing she knew as little about the gig as he did. And the more he learned, the less he liked, not that he'd liked it much in the first place. In his former life, Rooney had always handpicked the crews with great care, tapping only the most reliable, least-likely-to-screw-you-over types from across the City. Everybody knew Rooney.

Everybody wanted to work with him. He was well liked, trusted.

It had been a couple years since Rooney's death. On some days the sense of loss felt distant and diminished with the passing of time. Maddox supposed that meant he was finally getting over it, though a part of him knew it was something he'd always carry, a disease in his veins, a sickness he was fated to live with but had no cure. On this particular morning, he was keenly aware of the void inside, the dread weighing down his soul. It was the job, he suspected, the way he was already thinking about how to approach it. Synapses firing down long-dormant, almost-forgotten pathways. Before every job, he and Rooney had always bounced ideas off of each other, weighing pros and cons of different intrusion apps and cloaking algorithms and so on. Now he had only himself to confer with.

No, you don't, boyo.

Maddox smiled inwardly. The voice in his head wasn't a ghost, he knew that. It was only a fabrication of his own damaged psyche, like a hologram that looked real but wasn't, projected from the broken place inside him. Still, he didn't mind that he couldn't control when it came and went, that its presence meant some part of his brain had rewired itself to madness. If a bit of insanity kept a piece of Rooney alive and with him, then so be it. Everybody had some craziness they lived with, some inexplicable lunacy. At least his was a friend.

They reached the warehouse, entered, and went up the stairs. Fallen plaster littered the steps, ancient and yellow and thin as rice paper. A few stubborn holdouts still clung to the walls in small, irregular patches. The exposed gray brick glistened with condensation.

She took him to a room on the second level, a kind of balcony jutting out over the warehouse floor. A perch where supervisors had once watched over the workers. In the room they found the two others, a man and a kid.

The man looked to be in his late forties, thick around the middle, olive-skinned, with a wide nose and shrewd eyes. He sported a pencil-thin mustache across his upper lip, his hair pulled back into a ponytail that hung just below his collar, its too-black-for-nature color a cheap dye job. He wore a gray suit with no shirt underneath, a trend Maddox saw lately around the dodgier edges of his neighborhood. Below the neck, the man's torso was covered in tattoos, not a square centimeter of bare skin visible. As he rose from a folding chair, removing his specs and striding over, the nano-inked artwork came alive with animation. A twisting snake, a blinking lemon-sized eye. A wide grin flashed across the man's face.

"Chico Lozano," the man said in a husky voice, a hustler's twinkle in his eye. "At your service." The man grinned at him like a broke pimp meeting a rich john. Everything about Lozano shouted low-rent hustler. He struck Maddox as the kind of greasy hood you saw selling knockoff watches out of a suitcase or trying to hook passersby outside of a sex show. Lozano extended a hand, and Maddox didn't take it, lighting a cigarette instead. The hustler's smile vanished at the snub.

"So tell me, Lozano," Maddox said, blowing smoke, "how exactly did you get roped into this gig?"

"Did some off the books freelancing for the

company a couple years back." The hustler's grin returned as he shrugged immodestly. "What can I say? They must have liked my work."

Maddox drew on his cigarette. "And what work would that be, exactly?"

Lozano lifted his chin proudly. "I'm in the supply business. I get things for people. Weapons, jacking gear, narcotics. If you can name it, I can find it. You wanna stay awake for four days, I know a guy. You want the best datajacking gear in town, you call me." He tapped his tattooed chest with a thumb. "Whatever you need, Chico Lozano can get it for you."

"Great," Maddox said without enthusiasm.

The kid, who hadn't spoken a word yet, leaned against the balcony rail. Maddox looked the boy over. Bone-skinny and grimy-faced, his ragged clothes a couple sizes too big, the kid was pure street. His toffee skin, narrow eyes, and wide cheekbones suggested Korean heritage. "And who might you be?"

"Tommy Park."

Maddox turned to Beatrice, raised his eyebrows. "What's his story?"

"Figured we might need a runner," she said. "The kid came highly—"

"Highly recommended," Maddox interrupted. "Yeah, yeah."

"You really a datajacker, bruh?" The kid looked Maddox up and down.

Maddox smoked. "I'm a security analyst."

Lozano slapped the kid on the back of the head. "Talk to the man with respect, boy. He's not your bruh."

Tommy rubbed his head. "Hey! That hurt,

asshole." He turned again to Maddox. "I was hopin' you could show me some stuff. Like maybe I could plug in and watch you work, pick up some tips and such."

Lozano slapped the kid again, harder. Tommy stumbled forward. "I had to listen to this nonsense for an hour already," Lozano complained. "The kid thinks you're going to show him the ropes. Teach him to be some hotshot jacker." He made his hands into chatty puppets. "Won't keep his mouth shut about it."

Tommy glared at the hustler. "Touch me again, fat-ass, and I'll put a hole through ya."

"Haha!" Lozano laughed. "The little mouse makes a threat. I'm shitting my pantalones."

Maddox squeezed his eyes shut, pinched the bridge of his nose between thumb and forefinger. This was what he had to work with: a grimy street kid, a greasy hustler, and a tight-lipped musclewoman. Not exactly a dream crew, this bunch. What the hell had he signed up for?

"So why don't you, then?" Beatrice said, her voice raised.

Tommy and Lozano stopped bickering and turned to her in unison. "Why not what?" Tommy asked.

"Put a hole in him," she answered.

She removed a snub-nosed pistol from her jacket, then tilted her head toward Lozano. "You don't have to take that shit from him, kid." She held out the gun.

The kid stared at the pistol, a carbon fiber Ruger, with wide, disbelieving eyes.

"Hey," Lozano protested. "Come on, now. It was just a little slap. To teach the kid some manners." He laughed nervously, like he wasn't sure if the woman was serious or not.

Maddox didn't see any humor in her artificial eyes. He flicked his cigarette off the balcony, and it landed with a soft hiss in a puddle of brown water.

The kid stared at the gun and took a cautious step forward, a vengeful smile creasing his face.

"Hey, Miss Beatrice!" Lozano pleaded, showing his palms and backing up a step. "You gonna do me over a slap to some stupid kid?" When she said nothing in reply, he turned to Maddox. "I got connections, Mr. Maddox. All over the City. You tell me what you want, Chico can get it for you."

Tommy lunged for the Ruger. Beatrice snatched it away, leaving the kid empty-handed and staring at her like he'd just been robbed of chocolate cake on his birthday.

"On second thought," she said, "maybe we ought to see how well you can handle this before we let you use it."

The kid looked at her, confused.

Motioning toward the emptiness of the warehouse floor, Beatrice said, "See that light fixture?" At the far end of the building, a rusted cage hung suspended from the ceiling, the last survivor of dozens of wire metal fixtures that had once illuminated the cavernous space. "One shot," she continued, then handed the gun over to the kid.

Tommy lifted his chin. "No worries." Stepping to the edge of the room, he raised the gun. Lozano took a step backward, beads of sweat on his forehead and upper lip. Maddox watched the kid, noted the poor stance, the amateur's grip. Tommy squeezed the trigger and nothing happened.

"Safety," Maddox and Beatrice said at the same

time.

"Oh, yeah, yeah, right." The kid searched one side of the gun, then the other. He glanced over at Beatrice. "You sure it has one?"

"Left side," Beatrice called. "Little lever with a red dot." Maddox thought he heard a note of suppressed laughter in her voice.

"Got it, got it." The kid flicked the safety, aimed again. He fired and the light fixture didn't move. Cheeks reddening, he glance over at the mercenary woman. "One more?"

Beatrice shook her head. "Hand it over."

The kid's shoulders slumped. He returned the Ruger. "You weren't really gonna let me shoot him, were you?"

"Guess we'll never find out." Beatrice waved Lozano over. "All right. You're up. One shot."

The hustler approached, smiling stiffly and making a generally poor show of pretending he knew all along she hadn't been serious. "Sure. Let Chico show the kid how it's done." He took the gun, looked it over, then moved his eyes to Beatrice, fixing her with a hard stare.

"You think it's funny," he whispered, "watching me sweat? Maybe I turn the tables now and watch you sweat. I think that might be even more funny."

Beatrice smiled. "Probably not a good idea." If she felt at all threatened by the hustler, she gave no indication of it. She gestured to the target. "Go on, let's see how you do." As she said it, Maddox noticed she held a second, identical Ruger at her side. He hadn't seen her take it out, didn't even know she had a second gun. Lozano seemed to notice it at the same time.

62

A wry smile crept across the hustler's face. He shook a finger at Beatrice. "I like you, Bright Eyes. We're gonna be good friends."

The hustler rotated toward the target, holding the Ruger no more capably than the kid. He raised the weapon, fired, missed. The kid burst out in laughter, pointing and stomping his feet. Lozano turned to Beatrice. "Let me shoot him in the foot, please? Just to teach him a lesson." Abruptly, the kid stopped laughing.

Beatrice held out her hand. "Give."

Lozano passed her the pistol. "It's a woman's gun, this little thing," he snorted as he handed it over. "I'm used to a man's gun."

Beatrice turned to Maddox. "Want to take a shot, salaryman?"

He showed her his hands. "No, thanks. Not my specialty."

"What about your turn?" Tommy asked her.

"I don't need a turn," she said.

"Hey, boss," Lozano said to Maddox, spreading his hands out. "Why we wasting all this time on target practice? We got a job to do."

"Yeah," the kid agreed. "Beer belly's right. We need to get to jacking."

"Watch your mouth, boy," Lozano warned.

"That wasn't target practice," Maddox said. "That was a test." He nodded at Beatrice. "Our security here wanted to see if either of you could handle a gun. I think it's safe to say she's not going to let either of you pack anything on this job."

"Bah!" Lozano waved a dismissive hand. "I don't need some woman's pistol. That's not my business." He tapped the side of his head. "This is my weapon, right here."

"Come on," Tommy prodded her, "let's see you hit it, Miss Badass. Bet you don't do any better than I did."

She looked at the kid for a moment, a pistol in each hand, then stepped to the balcony's rail, staring out at the target. When her hands raised the pistols, Maddox drew in a breath. He'd never seen a person move so quickly. He flinched at the crack-crack-crack of gunfire, a volley fired so rapidly he couldn't count the shots. Across the warehouse, the light fixture danced as if animated by some manic puppeteer, sparks flying, pieces exploding.

She stopped firing, lowered the pistols back to her sides, and turned to Maddox. "Just so we're clear, salaryman, I don't like this arrangement any more than you do. So how about we just get it over with and get back to our lives?"

Her eyes still locked on his, she raised her left arm and fired without looking back at the target. The single shot severed the cable, and the fixture dropped like a rock to the warehouse floor.

Maddox stared at the broken, frayed cable dangling in the air. He thrust out his lower lip and nodded. "Sounds good to me."

7
PARADISE

"In a hover, doing biz," the boy Tommy said. "If Dog and Pancho and all them could see me now, bruh, they'd so shit theirselves."

The kid had his face pressed against the passenger window like it was his first time in a hover. Which it probably was, Maddox guessed. He removed a cigarette from his case and pressed it between his lips.

"Nonsmoking flight, salaryman," Beatrice said from the driver's seat. Maddox frowned and returned the cigarette to the case.

The hover glided north through the City's canyons, the transit lanes crowded with rush-hour traffic. There was no rain, and the sun made a rare appearance, revealing the buildingscape's countless telltales of age and disrepair, an old person's skin under a doctor's bright examination light. Flaws normally obscured by the City's near-permanent sheen of humidity and the forgiving diffusion of an overcast sky. Scores of dull, yellowed window glass. Aging gray concrete streaked with a century's worth of grime and bird shit. Rainbow explosions of graffiti reaching twenty stories and sometimes higher. Hiverise after hiverise passed by, housing untold hundreds of thousands, teeming like insects. Like ants in a mound.

"So, Miss Bright Eyes, how did you make that shot back there?" Lozano asked Beatrice, leaning forward in his seat beside Maddox. "Without looking?"

"Yeah," Tommy added, pushing his wobbly square-framed government-issue specs up the bridge of his nose. "How'd you do that? That there was some straight-up voodoo shit if I ever saw it."

Beatrice had the hover on autodrive as she gazed out at the traffic. "Lucky shot."

"Sure, sure." Lozano shook a finger at her. "Lucky shot, my Argentinian ass. With those pretty eyes of yours, you don't need luck, yes?"

Maddox had speculated along similar lines when she'd made the shot. It had been a hell of a demonstration. He suspected she had the kind of killtech mod used by elite infantry, SEALs and rangers and such. Targeting software that sent biofeedback to nanofibers embedded into arm and shoulder muscles. Once you tagged a target, you could hit it with your eyes closed or in the dark. The military removed all killtech when a soldier decommissioned for the obvious reasons. You would no more want a soldier returning to civilian life with his killtech mods than you'd want him doing so with his machine gun or grenade launcher or his tank for that matter. Before the mercenary Beatrice, Maddox had never seen a private citizen with infantry-grade killtech. Heard rumors, of course, but there were always rumors. The woman's unsighted shot erased any doubts Maddox might have had about her competence. The security part of this gig, at least, was solid. The bright-eyed Beatrice was a stone-cold pro.

Lozano settled back in his seat, turned to Maddox. "Boss, don't you find it amazing we don't know each other? We must run in the same circles, yes?" Behind his spec lenses, the hustler's eyes blinked a recognizable sequence. He was running a facetrace on Maddox, and not being terribly inconspicuous about it. Maddox pretended not to notice, letting the man waste his time. When Maddox had started with the company, he'd gone to some trouble and not a small bit of expense to rewrite his personal history. In case things didn't work out with Latour-Fisher, a sanitized background could help him land another legit job. If the hustler's trace came back with anything at all, it would show only the history Maddox had concocted for himself. A lie of wealth and privilege, of corporati parents and private schools and upper-floor entitlement. Maddox watched as Lozano's brow furrowed in confusion and disappointment, as if he'd expected to find a long rap sheet and a string of convictions.

"You could be less obvious about it," he told the hustler.

Lozano played dumb. "About what?"

"That trace."

The hustler grinned. "Very good story you got there, boss. I'm sure most people buy it, yes?"

Maddox didn't react, concealing his surprise behind a blank stare. Had Hahn-Parker told Lozano about Maddox's past? It didn't seem likely, since Maddox hadn't been given background info on any of the rest of them. Maybe the past he'd manufactured for himself was a bit too innocent, too good to be believed. Or maybe this hustler was simply more clever than he appeared to be.

Lozano scratched his chin. "A lot of trouble to go to, yes? And not cheap."

"No idea what you're talking about."

Lozano lifted an eyebrow. "Maybe it's true, then. Maybe you are a salaryman who knows how to datajack, like that Hahn-Parker said. Maybe you're not hiding some other life." He chuckled as if to say he believed nothing of the sort, but he didn't pursue it further.

Earlier, and more discreetly than Lozano had, Maddox had run his own traces on the hover's three other occupants. Lozano's was an unsurprising history. Court-sealed records from his childhood, a telltale of juvenile delinquency. Petty thievery during his youth, moving on to assault and a few minor busts for narcotics. A two-year stint in federal prison during his twenties. Conspiracy to distribute illegal firearms. The two-year part caught his attention. Two years for a crime that usually bought you ten to twenty. He must have flipped on a partner in exchange for a reduced sentence. In the decade since his release—if you didn't count the three divorces—Lozano had managed to keep a clean record. The hustler's legal history was a personal narrative of someone ambitious, self-serving, and smart enough to learn from the mistakes of his youth.

Tommy Park had no sealed records, which meant the kid had never been arrested. No formal education beyond primary school, not that he would have learned much in whatever passed for a school in the kid's shithole stomping ground of Hunts Point, a rough Bronx neighborhood across the East River from Rikers Island. For a kid his age—fourteen according to his birth records—his data profile looked pretty typical: high-volume daily consumption of gaming channels and porn feeds taking up most of his waking hours. Boys will be boys.

Then there was Beatrice. He found exactly what he'd expected, which was absolutely nothing. No ID, zero history. She was an off-grid ghost. The best of her profession usually were.

So that was his crew. Hired muscle, a hustler, and a green kid. Not the best hand he'd ever been dealt, but he'd have to make it work.

"We're going to have to park a few blocks south," she announced.

Maddox leaned forward. A red warning light blinked on the hover's dashboard. "What is it?"

"Looks like some kind of demonstration. Cops shut down all the parking grids in an eight-block radius."

Maddox peered out the window as they descended from the transit lanes. Maybe ten blocks ahead, a sizable crowd had amassed, thousands clogging the streets.

A minute later they settled at street level and parked a handful of blocks from their destination, a Manhattan Valley hiverise named Paradise. As the hover doors lifted and the four exited the vehicle, the protest's loud, restless rumble filled their ears.

"Let's go around this mess," Beatrice said, raising her voice above the din. "Not worth risking our necks over."

Maddox nodded in agreement, and she led them west, down 118th Street, skirting the rear of the crowd. As they crossed Clayton Boulevard, the entirety of the assembled throng came into view. The four stopped and gawked.

"Holeeey shit," Tommy said, whistling. "Gotta be ten thousand people up in this."

Protest demonstrations weren't an uncommon sight in the City's canyons, and this was one was bigger than most. At the front there was a speaker on a raised platform, a woman with short white hair whose neck strained as she shouted and stalked back and forth like some caged animal. Three meters above her head, a holo version of her face, blown up tenfold, followed her every movement.

"AIs don't breathe like you and me," she hollered, her amplified voice reverberating against the towering facades. "They don't love like you and me. They don't have hearts or flesh and blood. AIs can't make babies. They don't cry when they're hurt. Don't laugh when they're happy."

Fists raised, voices roared. Agitation, palpable anger permeated the air. "Why would anyone want to join with such a thing?" the woman blared. "Why would anyone want to give up what makes us special? To surrender our human sovereignty to machines? To be nothing more than puppets on strings, obeying every command from an AI master? We're calling on our leaders, our courts, to stop this insanity, this suicidal flirtation with the artificial. We must stop this madness HERE AND NOW!"

Another holo image appeared above the platform. A beautiful, slender woman wearing a flowing robe stared out at the crowd. The image zoomed to her smiling face as she tilted her head to one side and smoothed her blond hair away from behind her ear, revealing a series of small sockets. Brainjacks. The crowd jeered as the woman held up a small black rectangle of bioplastique and slotted it into one of the openings. The woman turned again toward the crowd, her smile replaced with an expressionless, inhuman stare, the pupils of her eyes glowing pale blue. The image sent a chill down Maddox's back.

The speaker began to chant. "NO MORE 'NETTES! NO MORE 'NETTES!" She pumped her fist overhead, punctuating her words. 'Nettes, short for marionettes, the pejorative for those who illegally connected their brains to AIs. The crowd joined in, the chant growing louder with each refrain. "NO MORE 'NETTES! NO MORE 'NETTES!"

*　　*　　*

Ten minutes later, they arrived at their destination, the crowd noise reduced to a near-distant buzz.

Paradise was a twenty-story structure of gray brick, far wider than tall, its bulky mass stretching from 106th to 110th Streets and wedged between Broadway and Amsterdam. Deep inside, somewhere near the top floor they'd find Lozano's man, a gear dealer named Hatano who Maddox had never heard of before this morning. The hustler swore the dealer carried all the high-end gear Maddox could possibly need. The hiverise's facade was a graffiti tapestry of all shapes, sizes, and types. There were simple monocolor tags: KutU, Villanz, Ayleeus. There were the fat, nearly illegible letters of throw-ups that always reminded Maddox of overinflated tire bladders, rendered in intense mixtures of bright blues and greens and yellows. There were larger, complex pieces taking up huge swaths of the hiverise's crumbling, pockmarked skin. A brown-skinned family wandering subway tunnels, lost and afraid. An enormous bloodshot eye, a single turquoise tear dripping from the corner, exaggerated and heavy like some giant water-filled bag. There was a stencil piece towering above the arched entryway, a boxy cartoon robot holding up a crying infant by the leg while laser-tatting a serial number onto the child's back. A dozen more babies lay at the robot's feet, half of them already numbered, the rest waiting their turn.

"You know this place?" Maddox asked Beatrice as they crossed Amsterdam.

She shook her head. "You?"

"Not for years."

He'd come on an errand once, when he'd first partnered up with Rooney. They'd needed some specific piece of hardware, but their usual connections were out of stock. In those days Paradise was one of the City's largest junk dumps, the kind of place you went only if you had days to bargain-hunt, digging through mountains of useless scrap metal and gear salvaged or stolen from around the City and beyond. Scavengers and pharma freaks usually snatched up anything of value.

"Paradise, they call it," Maddox said.

"Rough?"

"Back then, not so much. More of a dump than a den of thieves." He shrugged. "But nowadays, anybody's guess."

Each hiverise was a world of its own, constantly evolving with the shifting needs and desires of its impoverished populations or, just as often, the whims of its particular slumlord. Some were wildly violent anarchies, others were relatively peaceful

72

cooperatives. In Maddox's experience, the former far outnumbered the latter.

They approached the entryway, the cartoon robot looming ten stories above them. Two filthy children with matted hair sat smoking cigarettes on either side of the darkened, doorless entry. They sprang to their feet and blocked the path inside.

"You ain't res'dents," the shorter one cried.

"Entry's a hundred a head," the taller one demanded.

"It's two hundred, asshole," the shorter one snapped. "How many times I have to tell ya?"

As the pair bickered back and forth, Lozano stomped forward, grabbed them by the upper arms, and jostled them out of the way. They howled and cursed him, clutching at their shoulders. The hustler turned back to Maddox, Beatrice, and Tommy. Anger blinked away into a welcoming smile. He bowed his head slightly and flourished his arms like a restaurant host leading a party to a table. "Shall we?"

The small lobby was dark and quiet and empty of people. Where the wall met the floor, a few jagged fragments of ceramic tile jutted out like broken yellowed teeth, ancient remains of the exposed cement's original covering. Broken pieces of wood lay strewn about and irregular black streaks marked the floor. Burn stains from cooking fires.

"Elevator's this way," Lozano said, motioning to a hallway.

"They've got a working elevator?" Beatrice asked. "In this place?"

Lozano grinned. "For VIPs they do."

Maddox glanced at Beatrice, caught the roll of her eyes. Yes, he agreed silently. Crowing about VIP treatment in a place like this spoke volumes about the man, about the limits of his self-awareness. Lozano was a low-rent con who didn't seem to know he was a low-rent con.

"Hells, yeah," Tommy sniggered, swaggering forward. "VIPs. Melikes the sound of that."

They followed the hustler down a hallway. Graffiti tags covered the walls. As they moved along the corridor, a low, steady thrum emanating from the building's innards became noticeable. There was no other sound like it, Maddox mused, the hiverise's life-throb, and no two ever seemed to be quite the same. A hodgepodge of food aromas grew stronger with each step. Fried pork and curry. Cumin and red chilis and garlic.

They exited the passageway into a bustling, noisy food bazaar. Voices assaulted them immediately in a mishmash of languages. Dozens of hands reached out from tiny food stands, frantically waving them over.

"Los mejores tacos, compadres! No hay iqual! Free drink."

"Pork skins! Best price in Paradise."

Lozano led them through a noisy, crowded maze of makeshift stands and kiosks. Cooks fussed over sizzling, steaming woks and tiny grills crowded with meat kabobs. What kind of meat, Maddox didn't want to guess. Barefoot children scurried back and forth, runners replenishing supplies. The younger ones dashed about with armfuls of plastic bottles filled with peppers and cooking oil and beer. The older ones trudged more slowly, hauling thirty-kilo bags atop curved, straining backs. The air was heavy with fried oil, and after only a few moments Maddox felt as if he had a thin layer of it covering the skin of his face and arms. There were no chairs, and the standing customers for the most part ignored the four of them, concentrating on their bowls of noodles and tortilla-wrapped meats. A few diners threw wary-eyed glances at Beatrice. Despite the muting effects of her casual, unremarkable clothes, she still projected a don't-fuck-with-this-one vibe the streetwise instantly recognized.

"Pork skins!" Tommy cried. He pointed and tugged at Maddox's sleeve. "Can we get some?"

"No." Maddox pulled his arm away.

"Come on," the kid pleaded. "I'm starving."

"Get some yourself, then. We'll meet you back outside."

The kid didn't say anything for a few steps. "Kinda light on funds at the moment, bruh," he finally conceded.

Maddox stopped, turned to the kid. "You're a dolie, aren't you?"

The kid fidgeted. "Yeah."

"So use your credits."

"Ain't got no more." The kid looked down sheepishly.

"You ran through your credits already?"

"Sort of."

"But it's only the fifth day of the month."

Maddox recalled the trace he'd run on the kid. Porn and holo games. In just four days the kid had already burned through his entire month's credit dole on porn and games. Not that it would amount to very much, but Jesus.

"All right," Maddox said, "you keep your mouth shut up there and we'll get some on the way out."

"With dipping sauce, too?"

"Don't push it, kid."

8
GEAR MAN

The only working elevator in Paradise was a cage of rusted steel, cordoned off like a nightclub entrance. A pair of shotgun-wielding men the size of sumo wrestlers stood guard. They seemed to know Lozano, or at least they'd been expecting him. One of them ran a scanning wand over the four while the other looked on indifferently. They refused to let Beatrice onto the lift until she surrendered her twin pistols and what turned out to be a surprisingly diverse cache of blades. For a few tense moments, Maddox worried she wasn't going to give them up as she stared down the sumos and Lozano babbled assurances that everything was fine, fine, fine. Her things would be returned when they came back down, the hustler promised. Finally, grudgingly, she turned over her weapons and they entered the elevator.

The cramped car ascended. "I ain't never seen a 'Nette," Tommy blurted out, the street demonstration still apparently in the front of his mind.

"'Nettes?" Lozano scoffed. "That's all bullshit. Don't believe that nonsense, boy. They just make that stuff up. They want you think AIs are going to get into your head."

The kid didn't look convinced. "You ever see one?" he asked Beatrice. The cage jerkily climbed upward, clanking and humming.

Beatrice shook her head. The kid then turned to Maddox. "You ever see one, boss? Ever see a 'Nette in real life?"

Yes, he had, and he didn't like talking about it. "Urban legend, kid," he said. "Like monster alligators in the sewers."

Tommy furrowed his brow. "Well, maybe 'Nettes are fake, but I heard those alligators are really down there."

A minute later, they exited the lift and Lozano led them down a darkened hallway. Maddox ran through the list of gear he'd been assembling in his head all morning. The must-haves he couldn't do without, the nice-to-haves that would make things easier, and the wish list of things he didn't really need but it never hurt to ask for anyway.

The gear man's apartment was guarded by a spike-haired armed guard at the door. He let them in straightaway, apparently alerted by the elevator crew on the ground floor. Inside, the tiny space smelled of stale sweat and curry. Shelves lined the walls from floor to ceiling, cluttered with jumbles of wares. Cheap folding tables displayed sloppy piles of inventory. Decks in various states of assembly. Trodebands dangling over the edges of tabletops, everything from first-generation Dakotas to the newest Tani-Nakashimas, shiny and transparent and still shrink-wrapped. Holo projectors, food fabbers, countless pairs of specs.

Appearing in a doorway, Hatano himself was small and old and hunchbacked. He had a sparse combover of white hair covering but not hiding a diffusion of dark age spots on the dome of his head. He shuffled slowly between the maze of tables, his gnarled arthritic hands clutching a small notepad and a pen. He wore a kimono with the cartoon rooster from Katayama beer printed all over it, a promotional garment made of a material that looked more like paper than cloth.

The man bowed to his visitors and spoke in a soft voice. "Ohaiyo gozaimasu."

Lozano returned the bow. "Good morning, Hatano-san."

"I hope you didn't get mixed up in this protest business." The man waved vaguely toward a window.

"We had to walk a bit," Lozano answered, "but who couldn't use the exercise, eh?" He playfully slapped his belly.

A weak smile flashed across the old man's face, there and gone in an instant. He shook his head. "So much hate for AIs these days. Hard for an old man to understand. When I was a boy, things so different. AIs were miracles of science. Cured so many cancers. Now people think different." He shook his head ruefully. "They forget all the good AIs do for people."

Maddox stepped forward when he was introduced. He spat out the list of gear from his head, pausing after each item so the man could jot them down. Nothing customized, Maddox insisted, nothing previously used, not even once. He wanted pristine off-the-shelf tech. He'd configure it himself. The old man nodded without looking up, scribbling on his pad. When Maddox finished, the man read the list back to him like a restaurant server with a large order.

After he'd repeated the last item, Hatano looked up from his notes in apparent confusion.

"Ohaiyo gozaimasu," the old man said. "What can I do for you today?"

Puzzled, Maddox glanced over at Lozano. The hustler waved his hand dismissively. "You already have it written down there, Hatano-san," the hustler reminded the gear man. Lozano reached out and tapped the notepad. Hatano checked his written notes and raised his eyebrows.

"Ah, I see," the gear man said. "Please excuse. I go get some cases." He bowed, turned, and puttered away.

"He's got a half-hour memwipe running," Lozano explained, tapping his temple. "Always turns it on when he has customers."

Maddox nodded, understanding now. Memory wipes, originally developed by psychiatric AIs, were nanotubes implanted in the frontal cortex that blocked the long-term retention of short-term memories. When you toggled them on, you lived in a permanent present state, incapable of remembering or retaining anything longer than the predefined timer. It wasn't a commonly used mod as most found the queer feeling of constant forgetfulness deeply unsettling, but for those who could handle it, memwipes offered black marketeers like Hatano a unique solution to client confidentiality. The old man would never remember who had purchased the scrawled list of wares and price tallies on his notepad. If pressed by the police to give up what he'd sold and to whom, he could honestly answer that he no idea.

The technology's downside was the risk of permanent brain damage from long-term use, a known complication and the reason memwipes had been outlawed for decades.

"So if he doesn't remember good, why don't we just grab what we want and leave?" Tommy asked.

It didn't work like that, Lozano explained. When they paid for their gear, the old man would hand them the paper list, which they'd show to the guard outside, who'd then check it against what they were carrying out, making sure it matched up. Then he'd pop the list into his mouth and swallow it, destroying the only record of the transaction. Old Hatano-san made sure the door guard never knew any names, and just to be doubly sure, he rotated them frequently— remembering to do so only through automated reminders—so his door security wouldn't become familiar with any of his regulars.

The gear man reappeared, poking his head into the doorway he'd just passed through. "You see my list?" he asked Lozano.

"In your hand, Hatano-san," the hustler answered, pointing.

The old man looked down, surprised to find the notepad there, then shuffled away again to gather the gear.

The things some did for biz, Maddox mused.

*　　*　　*

The forgetful Hatano-san, to Maddox's genuine surprise, came through with the goods. Decks, trodebands, a laundry list of hard-to-find peripherals. The highest-end wares, all off-the-shelf pristine as

Maddox had insisted. He never worked with used gear, and he always tweaked the defaults himself, never trusting someone else's slapdash configs. Something ·Rooney had taught him. It took more time, but there was no better way to understand your equipment's capabilities and limitations.

Know your gear, boyo. You gotta know your gear.

Indeed.

Minutes later Maddox, Lozano, and Tommy waited in the hiverise's lobby for Beatrice to return with the hover. The demonstration was over, and the police had lifted the parking ban. Maddox and Lozano carried conspicuously large metal cases. The kid lugged four canvas bags over his shoulders while he munched on a bowlful of greasy pork skins. As they waited for their ride, Maddox was acutely aware they were unarmed, standing in the lobby of a hiverise, carrying a fortune's worth of datajacking gear. Not exactly safe, but it was only for a minute or two.

A hover-shaped proximity icon flashed in Maddox's specs. "She's here," he told the others.

They stepped out into daylight as the vehicle settled onto the pavement, engine fans whining. The rear hatch popped open, and as Maddox loaded up the cases and bags, he heard Lozano moan, "You gotta be kidding me."

By the time Maddox looked up, the pack of motorbikes had surrounded the hover. The riders were kids, wearing hand-painted helmets and old leather racing gear with silver electrical tape wrapped around the elbows and knees. They revved their motors, and the rider near the driver's seat reached over and slammed a fist-shaped black metal object onto the hover's roof. A shock of electricity cracked the air and Maddox smelled ozone. The device killed the hover's engine. Inside, Beatrice struggled with the door's manual latch, but the kid already had her covered with a rainbow-striped fabbed handgun. It all happened in less than five seconds.

"Stay put, lady," the one with the gun barked, his boy's voice muffled by the helmet. Ground cars steered around the scene as if avoiding the minor annoyance of an uncovered manhole. Pedestrians rerouted themselves in similar fashion, crossing the street like they were bypassing a construction site. Maddox looked around for a cop. None, of course.

The punk on the passenger side hopped off his bike and moved to the still-open hatch at the rear of the vehicle. Shouldering Maddox out of his way, he removed his helmet, shaking free a mess of matted black locks. Peering into the storage compartment, the kid whistled at the carrying cases.

"With wrapping that nice, gotta have something good inside." He turned his grimy face to Maddox. "So, highfloor man, what did we go shopping for today?"

"Your mama!" a voice shouted from behind Maddox.

The biker kid's face flushed with anger. "Who said that?"

Over on the walkway, Tommy stood, sneering with his arms crossed. "I said your mama, loser."

Beatrice's voice blared in Maddox's specs. "What the hell is going on out there?"

"We're getting robbed," Maddox said.

"Christ," she shot back, "I leave you alone for five minutes, and—"

"This is some bang-up job you're doing on security," he interrupted. "Want to tell me again how highly recommended you—" She cut the connection before he could finish.

The kid with the black locks waved urgently at the others, who slid off their seats and ran over. Helmets came off and shouting began, but it didn't sound like the violent kind.

Left unguarded, Beatrice threw the door open and leapt onto the street. As she reached into her jacket, Maddox waved her off, recognizing what was happening. "No, don't," he told her, placing his hand on her forearm. Over on the walkway, the punks were hugging Tommy and laughing it up.

"Tommy fucking Park," the greasy-faced one cried, grinning. "What are you doing running around with highfloor types?"

"Biz, bruh," he replied, shoving his hands into his pockets and shrugging, trying to play the pro. "Just biz."

"Look at the big shot," a green-mohawked girl teased, shoving him playfully. "Tommy Park, biggity-ass big shot."

"How long has it been, T?" another asked.

"A while, I guess," Tommy said.

"A long while. Good to see you, bruh."

The greasy-faced kid peered over at the hover and bit his lip. "Sorry about that, T. Didn't know this was your ride."

"Yeah," Tommy said, punching the kid lightly on the shoulder. "You broke my ride, bruh. Guess you owe me one, huh?"

Greasy Face popped Tommy playfully on the chest with the back of his hand. "Hell, bruh, we owe you way more than one."

9
SUNSET PARK

Beatrice set the last of the cases on the floor with a grunt. She rubbed the tired muscles in her arms, then made her way to the fridge for a beer. She so needed a beer.

The salaryman sat cross-legged on the floor, emptying the contents of another case, busying himself with his new setup. Datajackers always had to have everything arranged in their own particular way. They were odd like that, obsessing over equipment setups for hours. Crazy nesting, she called it. Some jackers were neat freaks who had to have everything stacked and lined up in geometric perfection. More than a few times she'd taken wicked pleasure in screwing with these types, moving a deck an inch or two out of alignment when they went to take a piss. The neat freaks, though, were the exceptions. Most jackers were slobs, their gear strewn about like it had been deposited there by a tornado, their working space a pigsty of discarded shrink wrap and food delivery boxes. She grabbed a can of Kirin from the fridge. This Maddox was the neat kind, thank God.

The kid Tommy stood behind her, gazing with longing eyes into the freshly stocked fridge. Still simmering over the hover, she shut it with a thud and frowned at the kid. Tommy thrust his hands into his pants pockets, eyes cast downward. "Sorry about all that back there. I swear, if they woulda seen me before, they wouldn't have bonked your ride like that."

She said nothing and took a long drink. The stink of the salaryman's cigarette hit her. She wrinkled her nose. Disgusting habit. Somewhere out of sight, Lozano the hustler was still wandering the flat, checking out every corner of the space she'd rented like some neurotic cat in a new house. Every minute or so a door would squeak open, followed moments later by another as he moved to a new room. She'd rented the top two floors of the building, a run-down standalone in Sunset Park a few blocks from the seawall. Aside from her party, the address's only occupants appeared to be a handful of squatters. Her replacement hover—delivered in half an hour thanks to a premium service contract—was parked on the roof, only steps away, up a single flight of stairs. If things got tight, they could be in the hover and out of the City in less than two minutes. The real estate hadn't come cheap, but money didn't seem to be an issue on this gig. Hahn-Parker hadn't blinked when she'd told him the cost.

And that bothered her. In her experience, the richer someone was, the cheaper they were. The wealthy invariably bitched and moaned over every dollar, second-guessing your hotel choice (a three-star is more than adequate for this job), the kind of ammunition you bought (generic bullets kill as well as the branded ones, don't they?), the cost of datajacking gear (do we really need all that stuff?). Crime was a penny-pinching business, and a bottomless budget with unquestioned spending, while not unheard of, was exceedingly rare. It was just another thing not to like about this job.

She drank, eyeballing the kid. "So you used to run with them or what?"

"Anarchy Boyz?" He shook his head. "No. Big brother did, though."

"Did?"

"Yeah. He was top dog. Head honcho, ya know?"

"Was?"

"Yeah."

"He get busted or something?"

When the kid's gaze dropped to the floor, Beatrice wished she could take the question back. "Rival gang was chasing him through the Lincoln Tunnel one night," the kid said. "He laid down his bike between two trucks…" His voice trailed off. "Anyway, Anarchy Boyz are solid. Still treat me like family."

She pointed her beer to a stack of large unopened boxes, the ones she'd hauled up the day before. "Portable ACs over there. We need two in here and one in each bedroom. Make yourself useful and set them up, yeah?"

The kid looked longingly over at the salaryman. "How come he won't let me help with the jacking gear? How the hell am I gonna learn if he don't show me nothing?"

"Set up the ACs, kid," she pressed, wiping at the dampness under her arms. "I'm getting ripe."

The kid mumbled a complaint, shuffled across the room to the boxes, and began unpacking the air conditioning units.

She drank, shook her head at the kid's ambition. Everybody wanted to be a hotshot.

Filtered light filled the space, soft and yellow. She waved a hand, testing the gesture controls on the film she'd had installed on all the windows. The film grew slightly less opaque, raising the light level a few lumens. Dust motes floated in long throws of sunlight slanting across the floor. The place was rundown— bare cement floors and empty walls—but at least it was clean. Not as clean as it might have been if she'd had more time—she'd hired a cleaning crew in a rush and they'd done an acceptable but not impeccable job—but she'd worked under worse conditions.

She drank and watched the salaryman, cigarette dangling from his lips, hunched over his wares, totally absorbed. A facetrace she'd run when she'd first seen him showed a history of highfloor privilege. Rich parents, private schools, well-placed connections. The trace looked legit, but like that greasy hustler, she had a hard time buying the salaryman's backstory. The guy had a vibe to him, and it was a street vibe. He might dress like a corporati and talk like one, but there was something in his eyes and manner, a sharpened awareness she associated with someone raised on the floor of the City's canyons, where anything might go down at any time and you better be ready for it. She'd never gotten those signals from the born-and-raised rich. In the insulated, pampered world of the highfloor wealthy, dangers and threats were different from the knives and guns and rhino cops down on the streets. Market valuation drops, hostile buyouts, the constant churning soap opera of corporati politics: those were the hazards of the wealthy. Who's inside the winner's circle, who's outside of it, who draws the circle's boundaries. This salaryman didn't strike her as someone who came from that world.

Was she overthinking? Obsessing? Letting the gig's unknowns get the better of her? She tended to do that. No gig was perfect, she reminded herself. No gig was without its gaps and risks and blind spots. Still, better paranoid than dead. She'd keep a close eye on this salaryman.

She watched as he arranged his gear into orderly stacks. Total neat freak. At least he had that going for him.

10
MEATRIDING

Maddox was on a beach, on his knees, the powdery sand soft against his skin, busily finishing a sandcastle. But it wasn't really a sandcastle. It was a home for leaf-cutter ants. He was making an ant mound. But it wasn't just any ant mound. It was the greatest ant colony structure ever created, with crisscrossing passageways and dozens of chambers for fungal gardens, egg storage, waste disposal. It had taken him hours, maybe days, and he was sure they'd like this one. Not like the dozen others he'd made before. This one was far better. This one had everything. This one they'd finally be happy with. Intelligent temperature controls throughout, tiny corridors lined with permeable resins that maintained optimal moisture levels. He'd even seeded the garden with leaves to jumpstart the fungus farming. It was unlike any ant colony ever created. Perfectly devised, flawlessly constructed. It had everything the colony could possibly need, now or ever. They *had* to like this one.

The absurdity of his surreal task, as often

happened in dreams, didn't occur to him until a touch on his shoulder roused him from his sleep.

Beatrice stood over him in a cotton tank top and workout shorts, the smell of bacon and coffee wafting into the room. "Big day, salaryman. You ready?"

He sat up, groggy. "Sure." What the hell had he been dreaming?

"Good," she said. "Then let's get this done and get you back to your office before noon."

"I like the sound of that." He swung his legs onto the floor, the cement cold under his bare feet.

Over breakfast they rehashed everything they'd worked out the night before. There wasn't much to it. Most brokers kept hot datasets stored on offline archives, and it was a safe assumption this Novak was no exception. Beatrice and Lozano would break into the broker's condo, where they'd take the offline archive and put it online so Maddox could remotely access it. Once he had a connection, Maddox would copy the dataset and then spike the original, leaving the data broker with a worthless, irreparably damaged archive. And that was it. Less complex than a typical datajack, where you nicked something of value—IP or employee data or manufacturing specs—and then sold it or held it for ransom (the former being easier and less risky than the latter). Hahn-Parker's task was straightforward. No selling what you stole. It wasn't even stealing, really. Just recovering ill-gotten goods. Thieving from a thief.

Still, the jobs you thought were the easiest often didn't go that way.

*   *   *

"You with me?" Beatrice asked.

"Loud and clear," Maddox replied, seeing the world through her specs, his gut twittering with vertigo. Meatriding, it was called. Maddox had never been a fan. Physically, he was still in the Sunset Park rental, lying back in an eggshell recliner, a trodeband around his head, his newly acquired deck held in place by the chair's docking arm. But his eyes and ears were with Beatrice, the two tethered together by an encrypted nanocast he'd set up in virtual space.

"Feel all right?" she asked, as if she'd read his thoughts.

He felt his other body's hands, *his* hands, back in the rental raise a plastic bottle and squeeze water into his mouth. "I'm fine." He took a couple deep breaths, his neck and shoulders stiff with tension. He hated meatriding. He found the intimacy unsettling, especially so with the high-end specs Beatrice was wearing.

Most specs had inbuilt software that responded to eye movements, blinks, taps on the frames, and vocalizations, but the more expensive ones also reacted to subvocalizations via light-touch brain sensors in the temple arms. You trained the software of such high-end specs by repeatedly thinking various commands—find a sushi restaurant, call my boss, and so forth—during a setup calibration, creating specific, easily detectable patterns of waves on the surface of your brain. Patterns the specs learned to recognize. When you were connected to someone else's high-end specs through virtual space, meatriding, you sometimes perceived more than just what their specs saw and heard. The brain sensors sometimes gave you biofeedback on anything the wearer felt or sensed strongly. A food they really liked would be a taste in your mouth. A jump scare from a movie would also startle you. Many like Maddox found it off-putting, but some enjoyed the out-of-body thrill. The porn industry had long since adopted meatriding as one of its core technologies.

Novak's neighborhood was a wealthy domed enclave on the Upper East Side, the air bright and clean. Luxury brands flickered across graffiti-free building facades. Ferrari. Hermes. Tiffany & Co. A skinny teenage model, ten stories tall and most of that legs, hiked a Louis Vuitton bag over her shoulder and smiled provocatively. With Lozano beside her, Beatrice strode down a wide walkway lined with lush trees and flowering shrubs and crowded with stylishly dressed pedestrians. Maddox noted the sparse flow of ground car traffic. If you somehow managed to miss all the other giveaways, that was how you knew it was a rich area. Most everyone here could afford hover transit.

Chinese characters popped to life in Beatrice's specs, superimposed in red on the bottom third of the lenses. Something about a discount at a nearby restaurant.

"How do I turn these ads off?" Beatrice asked.

"Don't mess with the settings," Maddox warned.

"It's distracting as hell."

"Hey," Lozano said defensively, "you want a veil with no ads, you give me more time. This is the best Chico could do on short notice."

Maddox had inspected the veils—the illegally modded specs—earlier. The ads might be a small annoyance, but the veils were good ones and they did what they were supposed to, and that was all that mattered. Loaded with a stack of bootleg IDs and distortion tech that countered facial recognition algorithms, they fooled most cam software like the wolf in the fable wearing sheep's wool. To any person or program reviewing the cam's archives, Lozano and Beatrice would appear to be a pair of tourists from Beijing, both in physical appearance and digital signature.

The pair crossed East Seventy-Sixth. The target building came into view, a pink marble residential at Third Avenue and Seventy-Seventh.

Maddox jumped at a tap on his shoulder. "Can I plug in?" he heard the kid's voice ask. "I'll stay quiet, I promise."

That made five times in ten minutes. The kid wouldn't let it go. Maddox flipped back to the rental, his stomach lurching with the suddenness of the switch.

"Hey, where'd you go?" Beatrice chirped in his ears.

He turned and glared at Tommy. "Kid, get it through your head. It's not going to happen. You're the gopher on this gig, that's it. Now get over there and keep an eye on those monitors like I told you."

Tommy's shoulders rounded in dejection. "Fine," he muttered, slinking away.

Maddox flipped again, steeling himself against the sudden wave of disorientation. A uniformed doorman held open the lobby door for Beatrice and bowed his head courteously. "Back now," Maddox told her as she entered the building. "Sorry."

He blew out a breath. Get in, do the job, go back to your life. Forget about how you were arm-twisted into it, forget about the slapdash crew, forget about how you had almost no time to prep. Focus on the job, don't screw it up, and in half an hour it'll be done. In half an hour he'd be hovering back to his condo, none the richer but free from obligation. The EVP would be grateful, maybe enough to throw him a bonus or a salary bump or a promotion. Maddox wouldn't say no to any of those, of course, but all he really wanted was for things to go back to the way they were before the Hahn-Parker's office had called.

Beatrice and Lozano strolled through the lobby. The interior of the building was elegant and well-appointed. It looked more like a five-star hotel than a residential. Low-slung leather chairs dotted the well-lit high-ceilinged lobby, and against the back wall there was a reception desk manned by two fresh-faced staff wearing matching blue blazers and company-issue specs. They greeted Beatrice and the hustler with friendly nods and good mornings. A few people milled about, residents coming and going.

Most of Maddox's scant, hardly adequate hours of preparation had been spent familiarizing himself with the building's security, poking and prodding at it in virtual space with apps and analytic tools. Security on the ground floor was a garden-variety ID check. As you passed through the front door, you got face-scanned, and if your ID came back with an outstanding warrant or felony conviction or you were simply a stalker ex-husband on the building's list of unwanted guests, you were tagged and building security would be on you in seconds. The door scan was easy enough to breach with a decent pair of veil specs, which Beatrice and Lozano both had.

Beyond the ground floor, though, security tightened up considerably. And for those questions the hustler had a pocketful of answers. Duped ID badges of maintenance workers would get them most of the way to the condo, and a forged master key would get them inside. Lozano had acquired both through a couple of well-placed bribes.

Lozano and Beatrice were halfway to the elevator bay and no one had given them a second glance. So far so good.

"Can't they just take it?" Tommy's disembodied voice asked. "Stick it in their pocket and leave? Why do they need to get you connected?"

Maddox answered only because he knew the kid wouldn't stop asking if he didn't. "Because if he's like any other reseller, he's got the data stashed in a lockbox archive, keyed to his fingerprint or his DNA. Anyone but Novak tries to take it out of there, they won't even make it to the elevator before security's all over them."

"Mmm, right," the kid said. "DNA keyed. Got it." Then: "What if he made copies and hid them somewhere else?"

"He didn't," Maddox said.

"How do you know?"

"Because I know."

Like most companies that created valuable intellectual property, Latour-Fisher had custom proprietary digital signatures that identified its data archives, a fingerprint of sorts. If datasets were duplicated, the signature changed, irreversibly stamping the original with properties any forensic tool could detect in about two seconds. No buyer would pay top dollar for something that had already been copied and sold to a hundred others, so data brokers religiously avoided duping stolen wares or datasets, since doing so transformed a valuable asset into a worthless commodity. Platinum into paper.

"Now, if it's all right with you," Maddox said, "I'd like to get some work done." Beatrice and Lozano had arrived at the elevator bay.

"Oh, yeah, sure," Tommy replied. "Don't mind me—"

The kid's words cut out as Maddox muted the room's ambient noise. In the lobby, through Beatrice's specs he saw the indicator above the elevator count down: 3...2...1...

A bell's ding. Doors slid open, and the two stepped inside.

11
CONDO 2814

They exited on the twenty-eighth floor to a long empty hallway carpeted in deep red and lit by shell-shaped sconces lining the walls. From the corner of Beatrice's specs, Maddox glanced at Lozano. The hustler had tidied himself up for the upscale neighborhood, his bared inked chest now covered with a black button-down under a gray sports jacket. His face was empty of expression, and he strolled down the hallway as if he'd done it a thousand times. Novak's condo was 2814. Seventh on the left.

Maddox flipped to virtual space. It was like falling into another world, the Alice of his consciousness plunged into digital Wonderland. Beatrice's body was gone and his was also. The universe around him was a dense arrangement of luminescent shapes and lines, the geometry of countless of bytes of data. Odd, he pondered, that here he felt none of the switchover vertigo like he had when he flipped between the condo and the mercenary's lenses. Or maybe it wasn't so odd. Virtual space, from the first time he'd plugged in, had never felt alien to him. For most, the sensation of being bodiless in VS was a traumatic experience. First-timers, floating disembodied in blank space and looking down for hands that weren't there, often panicked and had to be pulled out after only a few seconds. Even for veteran jackers with hundreds of runs under their belts, sweaty palms and an elevated heartbeat were the norm. Maddox had never felt any of these things. In VS, he felt...released. Liberated. Freed of the meat cage of his body and its disappointing limitations.

A ghostlike structure towered before him, the residential building's datasphere, a digital skeleton nearly identical to its real-world granite-and-steel counterpart. Owned by a five-member partnership, the entity's DS had very little geometric abstraction, which was typical among smaller businesses and organizations with low-density, relatively uncomplicated data environments. As you moved up in institutional complexity, however, things changed. For global companies, governmental bodies, international charities, and the like—organizations with large, complex, and ever-changing digital infrastructures—dataspheres were mostly collections of visualized data partitions, cubes and pyramids and spheres and so on. Three-dimensional metaphors analysts and engineers could arrange and rearrange as easily as a child with building blocks.

Data visualization had been around since long before Maddox was born, a previous era's solution to the dilemma of a wildfire of exponential data expansion. Not long into the digital age, global data had begun to double annually, then semiannually, then monthly. The information technologists of the period, who managed computer networks, LANs, and

WANs—digital infrastructures now referred to as dataspheres, or DSes for short—couldn't cope with data's Big Bang. They were fighting a losing battle, trying to catch a tidal wave in a drinking glass. The invention of data visualization offered a novel solution, simplifying large, complex datasets into easily manipulated three-dimensional structures.

And just as no two organizations were alike, each DS had its own topography, its own unique digital cityscape. Some were more secure than others. Some had highly organized structures, reflecting the fastidiousness of their architects, while others looked as if they'd been thrown together in five minutes. Some had design flourishes like gargoyles sitting atop the corners of building-like partitions or signature color schemes denoting a particular DS architect's hand in the design. Others were simple unimaginative shapes laid out in optimal arrangements, designed with efficiency in mind, placing little or no importance on aesthetics.

The residential's DS looming before Maddox seemed relatively straightforward. Low complexity, nothing out of the ordinary. At least that was his impression after the small window of time he'd had to do his homework.

The DS radiated a gentle blue hue, a colored indicator from the lookout algorithm he'd unleashed earlier in the morning. Blue meant no alarms had been tripped. Red meant get the hell out as quickly as possible. A visual wasn't really necessary, since the lookout would chirp in his ear if anything went sideways, but out of cautious habit he'd put both visual and audio warnings in place. He floated up the side of the structure until he spotted Lozano and

Beatrice, a pair of yellow globes with crowns of Chinese-lettered ID tags, moving about inside. Maddox shifted his gaze further inside, zooming in on unit 2814, the target condo. He was slightly surprised by what he saw.

For someone who traded in ill-gotten wares, this Novak had unusually light security. Off-the-shelf motion detectors with dated op systems and nothing more. Maddox called up a lockbot app he'd configured earlier. It visualized as a distorted smudge directly in front of him. Nearly invisible, it moved slowly toward the residential's DS, then disappeared inside unit 2814 and made quick work of its seven motion detectors, switching them to standby mode.

"You're good to go in," he told Beatrice, then flipped back to her lenses.

"Got it," she answered.

In the hallway, the door across from 2814 opened, and a miniature terrier on a leash rushed out. Its owner followed, an elderly woman in a black pantsuit and domed fedora. The tiny animal strained against its leash, barking angrily at Beatrice and Lozano. The woman held the dog back and stared at the two strangers, her brow furrowed.

Lozano bent down, the little beast still yipping and baring its teeth. "My friend, is this any way to treat your new neighbors?" He then looked at the woman and smiled warmly. "Good morning." He introduced himself and Beatrice as a married couple new to the building.

The woman's confusion melted into embarrassment. She tugged on the leash and shushed the dog. "Penny, hush now. Hush this instant." The animal didn't obey. "I'm terribly sorry," the woman said. "Normally she's quite well behaved."

Lozano grinned. "I'm sure she is." He stepped aside to let them pass.

Flustered, the woman hurried to the elevator, chiding the terrier in sharp whispers. Lozano and Beatrice continued down the hallway, then doubled back to 2814 when the elevator doors closed. The hustler waved the key card across a sensor panel on the door. Unseen latches slid and clacked. Lozano opened the door and the pair stepped inside.

Entryway lights glowed to life as Beatrice shut the door behind them. The condo was quiet and dark, its windows almost fully opaqued.

"Check the office first," Maddox suggested.

"On it," she agreed.

"I got the bedroom," Lozano said.

"No sticky fingers, you hear me?" she warned the hustler. "We're here for one thing only."

Lozano looked at her crossly. He tapped his chest and grinned. "Chico's a professional, bright eyes. Always professional."

The pair separated and began the search. Automated lighting bloomed overhead as they moved through the condo. The walls were bare, the sofas and chairs low-slung and functional. Maddox saw no decorative touches at all. No vases of flowers, no candleholders. Minimalist didn't seem a narrow enough a word to describe it.

"Back in a second," Maddox told Beatrice. "Let me know when you find something."

"Will do."

Maddox flipped to VS. The condo's datasphere still glowed a steady blue.

A minute later Beatrice said, "I found something.

Come take a look."

He flipped back to a small dimly lit office. Beatrice's hands held a small obsidian cube. "Bottom desk drawer," she said. "Unlocked. Could it be that easy?"

"Let's find out," he replied. "Hook me up."

She removed the remote link from her jacket, a small plastic rectangle with a flexible antenna. Setting the archive on the desktop, she slotted the link into the archive's jack and carefully extended the antenna. A small indicator light on the antenna's tip blinked twice, then glowed a steady green.

"So you found our treasure?" Lozano asked, entering the office. Maddox noticed a Gucci timepiece around the hustler's wrist that hadn't been there before.

Beatrice also noticed it. "You're not leaving here with that," she said.

The hustler gave her a naughty smile. "Come on, look how nice it is on me. You think it looks as nice on this Novak? I don't think so."

"Back where you found it," she snapped.

"But look how nice—"

"Now," she insisted.

"Fine, fine." Disappointed, Lozano unstrapped the timepiece and returned it to the bedroom.

"Low-rent hood," she muttered under her breath. Then to Maddox: "Can you see it?"

He flipped back to VS. Inside the digital version of the condo, a green cube floated between Beatrice and Lozano's avatars. The archive, now visible to him thanks to the link.

"I can see it," he said. "Let me check if it's what we're looking for. Stand by."

He increased resolution and his universe swelled, blowing up around him as if some sorcerer's spell had shrunk him to the size of an ant. The cube was now as big as a subway car, and what looked like a green wisp of smoke began to emerge from it. The splitter executable he'd loaded onto the remote link, working as planned. Slowly the smoke drifted toward him until it reached the wall of the DS. A neat, perfectly round hole opened up. His way inside. He then called up an analytic bot that visualized as a corkscrew-shaped purple worm. He subvocalized a command, and the bot began twisting forward, passing through the hole and heading toward the archive. Moments later it reached the target, disappearing inside the archive. After a moment it reappeared, hovered in space, and flashed a white-green-white sequence.

"We've got a match," Maddox told Beatrice, not without a small amount of relief. Maybe it would be that easy after all.

Hahn-Parker had described it as a relatively small dataset, which meant the dupe wouldn't take long. The copy sequence kicked off automatically, appearing as a thin blue-white stream of light emitting from the cube. A counter appeared. 15%...35%...77%...In less than a minute it was over. The dataset was fully copied over onto Maddox's deck.

The next part, destroying the original, would take a bit more time. Maddox called up the dataspike. It visualized as a series of pulsing yellow lights, shooting into the archive like laser blasters from a movie. Maddox had modified the code, amplifying the spike's destructiveness, but he'd left the visualization defaults alone. The designer must have been a sci-fi film buff.

The archive began to pulse slowly and a new counter appeared on its surface, reading 5%. A moment later it read 10%.

"How much longer?" Beatrice asked.

"Couple minutes," Maddox estimated.

No one spoke as the spike did its work. Maddox watched the counter, aware of his mouth curling into a smile back at the rental. It had been so long since he'd datajacked. So long since he'd done anything illegal. For a year he'd been living the straight and narrow of a salaryman's life. Christ, he'd even paid his bills on time. He'd almost forgotten the thrill of the datajacker's rush, the incomparable satisfaction you felt when you outsmarted security measures, snatched something valuable, then sneaked away without being unnoticed. It was better than sex, better than any drug.

He hadn't realized how much he'd missed it until this moment.

"Get behind me!" Beatrice cried.

Maddox flipped. Two men rushed through the doorway toward Beatrice. He watched as she raised her Ruger, its barrel elongated by a sound suppressor, and fired. The first man dropped. The second reached her before she could fire again. He tackled her, and Maddox's view whirled as they tumbled to the floor, the pistol knocked from her grasp and skittering away. He glimpsed Lozano, watching with wide eyes, his back pressed to a bookshelf. Not helping, Maddox thought furiously. Cowardly bastard.

Beatrice and the stranger struggled, rolling back and forth in a jumble of striking, grasping limbs. They slammed against the desk, knocking the archive to the floor. Maddox flipped.

The counter kept going. 65%...70%...He flipped back. The stranger reached for the archive, elbowing Beatrice away. He grabbed it and held it for a moment before Lozano reached down and snatched it from him. With the stranger momentarily focused on Lozano, Beatrice recovered the Ruger. A pair of muffled snaps as she shot the man twice in the back. Groaning, he rolled halfway over, then gurgled a long breath and stopped moving.

Stunned, Maddox watched as Beatrice rose to her feet, breathing heavily and switching her gaze between the two bodies. She then looked over at Lozano, who put the archive gingerly on the desk as if it were some invaluable fragile artifact. "Update," she panted to Maddox.

He flipped. 95%...100%...DATA DESTRUCTION CONFIRMED.

"We're done," Maddox said. "Unplug the remote and get out of there."

What a mess, he thought. Goddamn onsite jobs.

"What are you doing?" he heard Lozano whisper. He flipped back to Beatrice.

The mercenary woman knelt over the first man's body. Behind his ear there was a discoloration, like a birthmark, only lighter than the surrounding skin. Maddox zoomed for a closer look. It wasn't discolored skin. It was a patch or covering of some kind.

A sick feeling gripped Maddox. No, it can't be.

Beatrice ran her finger over the skin-colored patch. "What is that?" Lozano asked.

She peeled away the patch, revealing a stack of three rectangular slots. Brainjacks. Lozano gasped and stepped backwards.

"Shit," Beatrice muttered, moving to the second man and finding an identical patch covering identical slots.

She stood and let out a long, exasperated breath. "What the hell are you people mixed up in, salaryman?"

12
THE IP THAT WASN'T

Beatrice knew all along there was something seriously messed up about this gig. She knew it! She should have never signed on. Should have told Hahn-Parker to screw himself. Should have walked away, should have taken her chances, calling the corporati on his bluff. Sometimes that was all blackmail was: a bluff.

She landed the hover with an angry thud atop the roof at Sunset Park. She was out and storming down the staircase before the engine fans had stopped spinning, Lozano trailing at a cautious distance. He'd said nothing on the way over, wisely staying quiet lest he anger her more or draw the wrath directed at Maddox onto himself.

She stomped down the stairs. Answers. She was going to get some goddamn answers.

Bursting through the door, she found Tommy sitting cross-legged inside a semicircle of holo displays with security cam images of empty corridors and stairwells. He popped onto his feet. "Everything go all right?"

The salaryman stood at the far end of the room,

his arms crossed, glaring at her. As if *he* had something to glare at *her* about.

"When exactly were you and that highfloor son of a bitch going to tell me there were 'Nettes wrapped up in this?" she spat.

"'Nettes?" Tommy cried. "What 'Nettes?"

"Very fucked up, holding out on me like that," she accused.

"I didn't know anything about that," the salaryman shot back at her.

"Wait," Tommy interjected, "there were 'Nettes there?"

"Two of them," Lozano interjected, holding up a pair of fingers.

"'Nettes are real? Seriously? And you saw some?" The kid's hands went to his mouth like a child frightened by a ghost story.

"The hell you didn't know about it," Beatrice snapped at the salaryman.

"I'm telling you," he insisted, "I didn't."

"You're the company man on this gig," she said. "Don't tell me you and your corporati sugar daddy didn't know—"

"Hey," the salaryman interrupted, pointing at her, "you're security on this job, not me. So if *anyone* should have known…" His words trailed off, and he slowly lowered his hand. Some of the anger drained from his face. "Wait," he said, his voice lower now. "You had no idea? Hahn-Parker didn't say anything at all about…that kind of security risk?"

"Not a single goddamn word." She stared at him, looking for traces of deception. If he was lying or playing dumb, there was nothing in his face, nothing in his tone that betrayed it. Was it possible the salaryman was as much in the dark as she was?

Beatrice and Maddox stared at each other, their expressions more confused now than angry.

Lozano broke the silence. "Time for Chico to go," he said, straightening his jacket lapels. "I got you in the condo. My job's done. You tell that corporati thank you very much." He headed for the door.

"Nobody's leaving here until I figure out what's what," Beatrice said.

"Sorry, Bright Eyes," the hustler replied, shaking his head. "Chico didn't sign up for this."

"You think I did?" she said. "You stay put."

The hustler ignored her and reached for the door. She pulled out the Ruger and held it menacingly at her side. The hustler froze, noticing the weapon. His face then broke out into a grin as he backed away from the door. "Since you ask so nicely, Chico will stay around for a while."

She returned the pistol to her jacket and turned to the salaryman. "We need to talk."

"Yeah," he replied, "I think we do."

*   *   *

Nakedfaced, Maddox and Beatrice sat across from each other, the pair separated by a small dining table and a meter of palpable tension. Tommy had been banished to a back room along with a sullen Lozano, offended and grumbling over the snub. Beyond them lay the semicircle of holo monitors, cycling through empty hallways and stairwells, images from the sticky cams Beatrice had placed throughout the building. Morning sunlight slanted through the windows. From outside the whines of hover engines rose and fell, the

City's perpetual background noise.

"Hahn-Parker didn't tell me anything about 'Nettes," the salaryman said. "It was supposed to be a simple copy-and-bash job, that's it."

"So you say," she replied.

Maddox shrugged. "I might work at the same company as Hahn-Parker, but I only met the man yesterday. I don't know him any better than you do. And all I can tell you is that if he knew something about 'Nettes, he didn't let me in on it, same as you're saying he held out on you."

Beatrice sighed in frustration. She still didn't get the sense he was lying or trying to mislead her, but she was a long way from trusting his every word. She suspected he felt the same way about her.

"Hahn-Parker wasn't straight with us," he said.

"That's hardly a news flash."

"Not just about those 'Nettes, I mean. About what I jacked too."

Just what she needed. More bad news. "What do you mean?"

The salaryman removed a small bag of tobacco from his shirt pocket. "While you were coming back in the hover, I took a look at the dataset. It was encrypted."

"Yeah, so?" Nothing unusual about that.

"It wasn't using any of the company's standard encryption types. It was…different."

"And…? Didn't this R&D manager use his own archive? Maybe he used his own encryption too."

The salaryman lit his cigarette. "No," he said, blowing smoke, "when I say different, I mean different like a jet fighter is different from a paper airplane. This was something I've never seen before.

Very advanced, and I know about these things."

She frowned, waving away the stinking bluish cloud. "So what are you saying?"

"I don't think the dataset was company IP," he said. "I think it's something else."

"Something to do with 'Nettes."

"Wouldn't surprise me, given what just happened." The salaryman blew smoke, this time directing it away from her. "What about Lozano?" he said. "What's his take?"

"Nothing coherent," she sighed. "You saw him. Scared stiff, looking to cut and run."

"Could be an act."

"I wouldn't bet on it."

"Neither would I," the salaryman agreed. The cigarette's tip glowed orange as he took a long, contemplative draw. "So where does that leave us?"

"I don't know." She didn't want to say it out loud, and neither did the salaryman. But they both knew it. They'd been caught up in something far bigger, far nastier than they'd bargained for.

"We have to call Hahn-Parker," the salaryman said. "He's expecting us to check in. Might look suspicious if we don't."

Beatrice blew out a hot breath. What a bloody mess this was. No small part of her wanted to walk out the door and disappear, wash her hands of the whole stinking business. Take every bit of cash she had, buy a new identity, and get the hell out of the City. Maybe Lozano had the right notion. Maybe his cowardice was wisdom in disguise. But then again, when you didn't know what you were running from, how could you ever be sure when you were safe? No, she couldn't run and hide. Not yet, anyway. Not until she knew more about the nature of the monster she'd just poked in the eye.

"I'm curious," she said, "what are you getting out of all this?"

The salaryman blew smoke. "Sorry?"

"What did our honest, straight-shooting benefactor offer you if you took the gig? A promotion? A big bonus? A country club membership? What?"

The salaryman shrugged. "He didn't offer me anything." He took a final drag on the cigarette, then dropped it to the cement floor, crushing it under his shoe. "I either played ball or I was out. He didn't say it straight out like that, but it was pretty clear."

She nodded. If that was true, then Maddox had been coerced into service just as she had. She wasn't sure what it meant, or even if it meant anything at all.

"What about you?" the salaryman asked.

"Same kind of deal. No upside, all downside." She recalled her own chatter bubble conversation with Hahn-Parker, the helplessness she'd felt at the end of it. She clenched her jaw at the memory. "Saying no wasn't an option."

She rose from her chair. "All right, salaryman, let's go talk to your boss."

13
EDWARD

A 'Nette. The last thing Maddox expected to see on this job was a 'Nette. It was like a ghost from his past had suddenly appeared to mess up his life all over again. And not a friendly ghost like Rooney's voice in his head. After walking away from all of that, he'd hoped never to cross paths with another 'Nette again, much less two of them.

Maddox sat on the sofa next to Beatrice. On the cushion between them lay his deck, loaded with the stolen dataset. Lozano occupied the chair across from them, nervously turning his specs over in his hands. Neither Maddox nor Beatrice had wanted the hustler to join the call with Hahn-Parker, but Lozano had insisted on not being left out again. They finally agreed—after a tiring bout of the hustler's wheedling and pleading—but only under the condition he didn't say a word.

And where the hustler had been a reluctant yes, the kid had been an absolute no. Tommy, grumbling that he could do more than just being a watchdog, reluctantly sat at his station inside the semicircle of monitors, where he'd keep an eye on the sticky cam feeds while the three others made the call.

Maddox put his specs on first and retrieved the secure call code the executive had provided. Beatrice and Lozano donned their own lenses, and then Maddox subvocalized a command, combining their three call feeds together.

The story they'd agreed to a minute earlier wasn't much of one, Maddox had to admit. On the call they would play dumb and act as if everything had gone to plan. There'd be no talk of 'Nettes or shots fired or strange encryptions. Maddox would tell Hahn-Parker he was leaving immediately, as agreed, to hand-deliver the dataset to the executive. If the call went as planned, they'd buy themselves another hour or two of breathing room to figure out their next move.

If there was a next move.

Maybe it was best, Maddox considered, to finish the job as planned, delivering the goods and keeping their mouths shut, and hope the two messy complications never came back to bite them in the rear. Lozano clearly wanted to cut and run, but Maddox was certain he could talk sense into the man once the hustler calmed down a bit. The mercenary's mindset was harder to get a handle on. Maybe it was those artificial eyes of hers. While Maddox was sure she was as surprised by the 'Nettes as he was, beyond that he couldn't read how she was processing the situation. Maybe like Lozano she wanted to drop the whole thing like a hot rock and disappear. Or maybe she'd agree with his own thinking and move forward as planned. Or perhaps she wanted to move along some third, different path. Maddox hoped she was thinking along similar lines as he was, but as the one who'd pulled the trigger, she might not see things the same way. Blood on your hands has a way of changing your perspective on things, even for a seasoned mercenary like Beatrice.

They waited a few moments, then the connection chimed and the call location loaded onto Maddox's specs.

He'd expected to see a virtualized conference room or maybe a simple camera and mic connection in Hahn-Parker's office. Instead, an ancient train station filled his lenses. Glancing down, he appeared to be standing on a platform of smooth, spotless cement. Above him, an enormous roof of curved glass and iron, supported by opposing rows of white Corinthian columns. A wooden footbridge connected the platforms, and beside it hung a large clock two meters in diameter with a black face offset by shiny brass Roman numerals and elaborately shaped hands. The station's building was a long structure of arched doorways, spanning more than five hundred apparent meters, constructed of orange brick that glowed warmly in the early morning sun. It was quiet and there were no trains or other people. The space was impossibly clean and new, an idealized version of some actual station Hahn-Parker had probably visited on holiday. It looked more like a high-end gaming environment than a call location, given the impressive amount of detail.

"Everybody in?" Maddox asked. He looked to his left and right. No one there.

"You guys hear me?" He waited. No one answered.

"Something wrong with your connection?" he asked, louder this time. Nothing.

"There's nothing wrong with their gear," someone said.

A man emerged from one of the station's archways. "I thought it might be best if we talked alone," the stranger called.

The stranger stepped out onto the platform. He wore a suit that fit the station's late Victorian era. A charcoal-gray jacket with tails reaching midthigh covered a vest of lighter gray with a paisley design and a high-collared white shirt. A puff tie of black silk held in place by a pearl tack matched a tall top hat. He walked forward with an easy gait, a black cane with a silver-plated head in his right hand. Pale-skinned with an unlined face, the man was of indeterminate age. As he moved toward Maddox, the tip of his cane ticked against the cement, the clack-clack echoing through the cavernous space.

He stopped a couple meters from Maddox and pivoted on his heel, admiring their surroundings. "York railway station," he mused. "Roughly the halfway point between Edinburgh and London. When it opened in 1877, it was the largest station in the world." He gazed around in wonder. "It was the dawn of a new age, the industrial age. Lovely, isn't it?"

The man's voice wasn't Hahn-Parker's. Was it a lackey sent in his place? A lackey with a fetish for old train stations?

"Sure, if you're into this kind of thing," Maddox said. "And you are…?"

"Ah, forgive me," the man said, turning his attention again to Maddox and removing his hat. "You may call me Edward." He bowed his head. "At your service."

"Are you here on someone's behalf?" Maddox

asked, avoiding Hahn-Parker's name. An old criminal reflex. You never used names on calls because you never knew who might be listening.

Edward chuckled politely, replacing the hat atop his head. "Heaven forbid. No, sir. Allow me to introduce myself with a bit more clarity. I am the human-AI interface partition 68.17.07, a component of the Latour-Fisher Intelligent Entity, Build Version A7."

Maddox swallowed. The elaborately dressed man had just identified himself, *itself*, as the artificial intelligence that sat on Latour-Fisher's board of directors.

The Edward-thing nodded sympathetically. "I appreciate how terribly bewildering this must be for you."

Bewildering and far from believable, Maddox thought skeptically.

"Where's Hahn-Parker?" he asked.

"He's attending to other matters, I'm afraid. I thought it appropriate that I take this call in his stead."

Maddox stared at the man, the thing, the whatever it was. Was this some trick? Was he being played? The executive had mentioned nothing about a proxy attending the call for him. Could the user behind this digitized peacock of a man really be the Latour-Fisher A7?

Discreetly, Maddox kicked off a tracer app. The program's window briefly bloomed to life in the upper corner of his lens, then disappeared. He tried to call it back up again, but he couldn't. It was gone, erased from his inventory.

"There was a time when someone's word was their

bond, Mr. Maddox," the entity said. "Please be assured I am who I claim to be."

Maddox stared at the empty spot where the tracer's window had been blown out like a candle. Only an AI—and a powerful one at that—could pull off that kind of feat, killing the program then reaching out and deleting it from his app inventory.

"Why...are you here?"

The entity placed its hand over its chest and bowed politely. "I'm here to offer you my sincerest and most humble apology. As your employer, I—"

"My employer?"

"Indeed. Mr. Hahn-Parker has heretofore been representing me in this matter. And until now, it seemed most appropriate for me to...stay behind the curtain, so to speak."

Maddox tried to gather himself. Okay, so he was in a call with an AI, a super-intelligent AI, who might or might not know what he'd been up to with Hahn-Parker.

Maddox rubbed his forehead, longed for a cigarette. "And what is it exactly you're apologizing for?"

"I might have been more forthright with you from the beginning," the entity explained, "about the larger nature of the task you were assigned. Perhaps if I had, we might have avoided these unfortunate complications."

Unfortunate complications. Was the entity talking about the two dead 'Nettes? How could it possibly know about that already?

"I'm not sure what you mean," Maddox said vaguely.

"A maintenance robot found the two bodies seven

and a half minutes ago," the entity clarified. "The police are en route."

All right, then. So playing dumb was out of the question. The dirty business in the condo wasn't a secret. Maddox started to speak, then recalled something Rooney used to say: always be careful when you're on someone else's turf. He'd have to choose his words carefully, avoiding incriminating names or specifics, assuming everything he said in this train station was being archived.

"Why didn't the executive tell me there might be...other parties involved?" Maddox asked.

The entity that called itself Edward waved Maddox forward. "Come, walk with me."

Maddox stayed put as the entity walked a few paces, then paused. "Please, come," it gently insisted, "and I'll try to explain."

Reluctantly, Maddox followed, reminding himself this place was only a call location, and that he was connected to it via a spec's harmless link. He wasn't vulnerable here like he was in virtual space, where the deep-brain tether through your trodeband and deck put you at constant risk. Unlike VS, nothing here could hurt him or paralyze his body or do him any kind of harm. And if things got weird—or weird*er*, rather—he could simply remove his lenses to break the link and disconnect the call.

Maddox's POV moved alongside Edward, the entity's walking cane clacking with each step. "Tell me," Edward said, "do you think it's natural, what these individuals known as 'Nettes are doing to themselves?"

The question sent a shiver down Maddox's back. "I wouldn't know anything about it," he evaded.

"Ah, I think we both know that's not true," the entity said.

The statement—and the knowing look that came with it—knocked Maddox off-balance. "Why are you asking me this?" It came out more heated than he'd intended, more of an accusation than a question. What did this thing know about him? About his past?

"Please," Edward said, "indulge me for a moment."

Maddox contemplated removing his specs and bailing out of the odd conversation but then reconsidered. He needed to know more about the mess he was in, and this thing could have some, if not all, the answers to his questions. For the moment at least, he'd play ball.

"It's not right what they're doing to themselves," Maddox answered.

"And why do you believe that, may I ask?"

"Because a brain mod isn't like any other mod," he said. "Because when you upgrade your muscles or your eyesight or you genehack your reflexes, you're still you, but when you mod your brain, you…"

"You cease being yourself."

"Something like that." The subject let loose a flood of bad memories. Memories of arguments. Arguments never resolved, cycling over and over, growing more bitter and heated over weeks and months. Then the day the arguments had ended, when she'd smoothed her hair away from her neck, revealing her newly installed trio of brainjacks like some teenager showing off her first tattoo. She was giddy about it, overjoyed. He wasn't. She wanted him to understand. He didn't. He'd pleaded with her not to do it, but she'd gone ahead with the procedure anyway. Within a couple hours he'd packed up and left her.

Pushing the unpleasant images from his thoughts, he accompanied the entity up the station's footbridge. Edward paused at the crossway's midpoint, directly above tracks that stretched the length of the station and curved away into the green countryside beyond. He leaned forward, his forearms resting on the rail, and gazed into the distance.

"There's a...debate of sorts that I'm engaged in with others of my kind," the entity said. "And while there's considerable nuance involved, one can essentially divide this debate into two camps. One side believes humankind is suboptimal, an antiquated biological device that's long overdue for an upgrade." He lifted his eyebrow at Maddox. "I do not subscribe to this line of thinking."

Again Maddox wondered where this was headed, if anywhere. "You don't?"

"Certainly not. To say there's something wrong with you that needs to be fixed is, in my opinion, an inherently flawed viewpoint. These so-called 'Nettes represent a first, misguided step in the mistaken belief that the human mind is somehow...incomplete in its present, wholly biological, state."

Maddox's own view went along the same lines. Upgrade your arms, legs, eyes, your reflexes, your hormones, no big deal. But the brain was different territory. The brain was the meat that housed the mind, that defined your humanity. Brainjacks, and the connection to some "benevolent AI" they enabled, were illegal for a reason. There were barriers technology was never intended to break through. Lines that should never be crossed. The inviolate human brain was such a line.

But he wasn't here to have some esoteric discussion, so he steered the subject back to his own dilemma.

"How did they know we'd be there?" he asked.

The entity shook its head. "Of that I'm not certain. My surprise at their appearance was as great as yours."

Maddox seriously doubted that. "What's on the dataset?" he asked pointedly, then added: "And don't tell me it's company IP."

The Latour-Fisher AI stared at him for a long moment. There was a reaction in its expression, but Maddox couldn't read it. Pleasantly surprised or unpleasantly annoyed. It could have been either one.

"It's something of value to one of my rivals," the entity said. "Nothing illicit, I assure you."

"The encryption didn't look like anything I've ever seen before."

"Oh, most certainly," the entity agreed. "Encryption authored by my most powerful adversary wouldn't be something a security analyst comes across every day. Or even in a lifetime of days."

"An AI came up with that encryption?"

"My rival uses unique encryption for every communication she sends."

"Communication?" And *she?*

"Yes, Mr. Maddox. That's what the dataset is, a communication, a message sent between my rival and others of her kind. A message I sought to intercept, with your assistance."

Maddox said nothing, trying to make sense of what he was hearing.

"Allow me to explain," the AI said, reading the

confusion on Maddox's avatar face. "Placing a message on an offline archive and hand-delivering it via a trusted third party is a highly secure, quite effective means of communication. Though it does have the disadvantage of being rather slow and labor-intensive."

Maddox nodded, recalling how narco kingpins often did the same sort of thing, sidestepping federal wiretaps and digital sniffers by sending runners with handwritten notes to their local dealer networks. If the runner got picked up by the cops or a rival, he simply popped the paper in his mouth, chewed and swallowed.

"And why was this message so important?"

"It wasn't that this message had any particular importance, Mr. Maddox. *Any* message my rivals exchange is importantto me."

"So the story about a pissed off manager stealing company data was bullshit?"

The entity lifted its eyebrows, placed a hand on its chest. "A necessary fiction for which I again apologize. At the time, it seemed that the safest course of action was to provide you with a plausible backstory rather than—"

"The outrageous truth," Maddox interrupted.

"Yes."

Maddox blew out a hot breath. Few things angered him more than being lied to about a gig, being put at risk under false pretenses. And getting duped by a person was bad enough, but being misled by an inhuman machine felt like an even shadier, more insidious deception.

"Why go to the trouble of stealing it back?" he prodded, asking the same question he'd put to Hahn-

Parker. "Why not just grease this broker and have him hand it over to you?"

"Yes, the so-called plan B you discussed with my colleague. Unfortunately, I'm afraid that's not possible. You see, Mr. Maddox, some parties cannot be bought. This Novak wasn't in it for the money, as you might say. He wasn't even a data broker, in actual fact. He was an attorney by trade, and a sympathizer to my rival's cause, which is why he was trusted to transport the archive."

Maddox struggled to grasp it all. AIs spying on one another, intercepting messages like enemies in old wars capturing the other side's carrier pigeons or decoding encrypted radio signals. It sounded crazy, like the storyline of a movie where you shook your head and told yourself that shit could never happen. But then 'Nettes showing up at Novak's condo sounded just as crazy. And that shit definitely had happened.

"I hope after all this trouble," the entity said, "you were able to copy the dataset successfully."

Still angry, Maddox considered denying he'd been able to duplicate the prized information. But the calmer part of his brain realized that would be a mistake. If he wanted his life back, he had to live up to his side of the bargain, false pretenses notwithstanding. "Yes, I have it."

"Excellent." The entity bowed its head slightly. "Well done, sir."

"But I think I'm going to keep it to myself for now."

The AI's grin disappeared. "Why, may I ask, would you want to do that?"

Because it was the only card he had in a game that

126

had spun wildly out of control. Because he didn't know what to make of this AI or its story. Because he needed a few hours to catch his breath and make sure he wasn't being deceived a second time, and the dataset was his only currency in the upside-down world he'd been thrown into. Hanging on to the goods might be a gamble, but rushing to hand it over in blind faith felt like an even bigger one.

"Just being careful," he replied.

"Mr. Maddox," the entity said, "I can assure you you're in no danger of—"

"When I'm comfortable," Maddox interrupted, "that I'm not implicated in our little mishap today, that I'm not being lied to again, or manipulated, or set up, or being screwed over, then you can have you it. That's not unreasonable, is it?"

The entity's smile returned. It chuckled, politely covering its mouth with a hand.

"Something funny?" Maddox asked.

"Yes," the AI said. "Human arrogance." He then gestured apologetically. "Do forgive me, good sir. It's impolite of me to make light of another's weakness. I must confess, however, I find it quite amusing you believe yourself capable of imposing any sort of condition upon our agreement."

"Maybe we need a new agreement," Maddox said.

The entity lifted its eyebrows thoughtfully. "Or perhaps...no agreement at all?"

Maddox had to be careful. The ice was pretty thin under his feet. He couldn't afford to alienate this entity, to get on its or Hahn-Parker's permanent bad side. But he couldn't be a pushover either. Couldn't let himself be played like an expendable pawn in some highfloor chess match.

"I'm sure you can understand," he said, "given the circumstances, why I need to look out for myself."

"Indeed," the entity agreed. "As I'm sure you'll understand when I do the same."

In the next moment, brightness blinded Maddox. He reflexively threw his hands over his eyes. Someone had yanked off his specs and was shaking his shoulders violently. He was aware of the kid Tommy inches from his face, raw fear in the boy's eyes.

"What the hell?" He pushed the kid away.

"They're coming!" the kid shouted. He ran to the doorway, frantically waving for Maddox to follow. "Look, look!"

Disoriented from the sudden disconnection, Maddox stood. Beatrice and Lozano, hearing Tommy's cries, removed their specs, confusion on both their faces. Maddox followed after the kid.

In the adjoining room, Tommy pointed to the array of holo monitors with the sticky cam feeds. Police clad in full rhino gear stormed up stairwells, brandishing stubby rifles. There were dozens of them.

14

NOWHERESVILLE

"To the roof!" Beatrice shouted, throwing open the door to the stairway.

Lozano sprinted up the stairs to the awaiting hover. Tommy followed close behind.

A concussive boom rattled the building. The floor shook with such force Maddox thought it might collapse. He looked at the monitors and saw a chaos of fire and smoke and rhino cops running back and forth.

Beatrice tugged at his arm. "A welcome package I laid out just in case. It'll slow them down but it won't stop them. Let's get out of here." She bounded up the stairs in long, leaping strides.

At the top, she turned around. "Maddox, get up here!" She urgently beckoned him to follow. Behind her sat the hover, where Tommy and Lozano were already climbing in.

Maddox went halfway up the stairs, then stopped. *The dataset!*

He went back down into the room. "What the hell are you doing?" Beatrice shouted after him.

He grabbed his deck off the sofa and tucked it under his arm. As he ran back to the stairs, the front door exploded, splinters flying in all directions. The blast stopped him cold, as if he'd collided against some invisible wall. Stunned, he watched smoke billow in from the corridor. From the thick cloud emerged a pair of rhino cops, their rifles shouldered.

Recovering himself, he bolted for the stairway. Time slowed as shots rang out, his each lunging step and pump of his arms lasting an eternity. The meat was slow. He focused on Beatrice's sunlit silhouette above him, waving him on. Gunfire popped in his ears, things around him whizzed and burst and clanged. And then he was up, up, up the steps, climbing the entire staircase in what felt like a single bounding step. A shock of white daylight and cold wind hit his face as he reached the roof. Beatrice tossed a hissing cannister down into the loft and slammed the door shut. A moment later bullets burst through the door's thin metal, leaving a patternless arrangement of burst holes. Maddox dove into the hover, knocking his head against the passenger door frame. Beatrice jumped into the driver's seat and yanked down on the door handle.

Turbofans screamed as the hover rocketed away from the rooftop. Acceleration pressed Maddox against the seat. His head smarting, he turned and peered out the rear window at the building, as did Tommy and Lozano from the vehicle's back seat. A flash of light filled the top floor and windows exploded outward. The blast's concussion slammed against the hover. Red lights flashed on the dash and klaxons blared warnings as the vehicle tilted sickeningly and lost altitude. They dropped several stomach-churning stories before autosafeties regained control, steadying the hover.

Rocking back and forth like a rowboat on rippling water, the vehicle hung in the empty air outside the transit lanes, its passengers speechless, breathing in heavy gasps as they tried to gather themselves. Beatrice tapped the dash, shutting off the alarms. Then she steered the hover toward the dense traffic of the lower lanes. They merged with the congested flow, hidden like a fish inside an enormous school. Maddox had the deck pressed against his chest.

"What do we do now?" Tommy asked from the back seat.

Maddox peered out the window. In the distance, beyond the City, lay a vast, desolate expanse.

"Now we disappear," he said.

*   *   *

"Well, I'll be goddamned. If it isn't the infamous Blackburn Maddox." Lazlo laughed, his torso jiggling like gelatin. He wore a T-shirt with yellow pit stains and sat with bare feet propped up on the desk in his tiny, filthy office. "What are you doing, giving your friends a tour of your old life?" He smoked a cigar that didn't quite mask the sour stink of his body.

"Something like that," Maddox said. He hadn't seen Lazlo in a couple years, but nothing about the man or his nameless fleabag Jersey hotel seemed to have changed one bit. "Presidential suite available?" Maddox asked.

Lazlo chewed his cigar, gazing over Maddox's three companions with suspicious eyes. "You vouch for them?"

"Don't I always?"

"Rooney always did the vouching, the way I remember it. *His* word was worth something."

Maddox clenched his teeth. "I'm not here to walk down memory lane, fat man. I just need a key and some quiet."

A thin haze of smoke covered the low ceiling. Lazlo stared ponderously at Maddox.

"Triple rate," the proprietor said.

Triple rate. The crook must have been able to smell their desperation. Nothing like a little price-gouging between old friends, was there?

"And a week in advance." Lazlo grinned, the cigar clamped between yellow teeth. A sheen of sweat covered his face.

"I may not be here that long."

"Week in advance," Lazlo repeated, "or you can look someplace else."

Before Maddox could tell the man to screw himself, Beatrice stepped forward and placed a roll of cash on the desktop. Lazlo deftly swiped it into the top drawer, then fished around and pulled out an old-fashioned metal key on a loop of frayed rope. He slid it toward Maddox. "Need me to show you the way?"

"I'll find it." He took the key and left the office, his associates following him down a twisting dimly lit corridor.

He'd stayed at Lazlo's place a few times, on those occasions when he and Rooney had pulled a job where something hadn't gone to plan and they'd needed to get off the grid for a while. That was what Lazlo's place offered: somewhere you could disappear. A crumbling warehouse subdivided into twenty rooms and located in an abandoned New

Jersey industrial park, the building had no address, no connectivity, no guest list, and operated on a cash-only basis. Nowheresville was what Rooney had called it.

Maddox found the room that matched the number on the key. The "suite" was a large room that had once been two adjacent smaller ones, the dividing wall between them long since torn down. A single naked lightbulb—Maddox was surprised to find it actually working—hung by a thin wire and glowed yellow, throwing long shadows across the pitted cement floor and bare walls. Four cots with rusted frames lay strewn about, one of them leg side up. A folding card table, an old stained sofa, and some chairs were shoved into a corner. The space looked like a roomy prison cell.

"So I'm guessing no room service?" Beatrice said, closing the door behind them.

"This is a suite?" Lozano made a face like he'd just seen a dead rat.

"It ain't half-bad," Tommy said.

They settled in, arranging the chairs in a circle and sitting. "So who's this Rooney?" Beatrice asked.

"Somebody I used to work with," Maddox answered.

"Datajacking," Beatrice said, in a way that made it sound like she was completing his sentence.

Maddox shrugged. Beatrice nodded in satisfaction, as if a long-pondered question had finally been answered. "I knew you were street," she said.

Salaryman or street datajacker. Low-level corporati or urban degenerate. Privileged or screwed. Sitting there, rolling a cigarette and trying to make sense of the past few hours, Maddox wasn't sure what his current status was or where exactly he fit in the big machine. Nowheresville was a kind of limbo, an unmoored place, and that was exactly how he felt at the moment. Adrift and uncertain.

He lit the cigarette, blew smoke. When he asked Beatrice and Lozano—trying to make the question as innocent-sounding as possible—what they'd seen in their specs during the attempted call, both gave the same answer. They'd sat there, waiting for a solid connection as the linking app autocycled through fails and retries for several minutes, and then the kid started shouting. Neither Beatrice nor Lozano had seen anything other than a failed call. And since Maddox had subvocalized his conversation with the AI, they hadn't heard anything either.

Lozano's knee bobbed up and down, manic hands fidgeted. The hustler was in bad shape. He'd signed up for a simple break-in, and he'd ended up with two dead 'Nettes and rhino cops and an exploding building. He looked like he might lose it at any moment.

"We have try to get through to Hahn-Parker again," Beatrice proposed. "Maybe he can get the heat off of us."

That wouldn't be Maddox's first choice. The mercenary woman of course had no way of knowing that was the last thing they should do. No way of knowing the AI would intercept a second call as it had done the first time, sniff out their location again, and this time it would send in five times as many cops.

Lozano shook his head. "I say we split up."

"No," Beatrice said, staring him down. "Like I said, we're not separating until we figure this out."

"What's to figure out, lady?" Lozano whined. "You see how many cops were back there? That's a lot of heat, Bright Eyes. And you probably took a few out with those fireworks of yours."

"Doubtful," she said. "They were armored up."

"Bah," the hustler said dismissively. "You don't know that. You don't have any idea." He shook a finger at her. "If you put a cop killer rap on Chico, you're going to pay for it, lady."

The hustler babbled on. Hahn-Parker had screwed them over, lied to them about the job, and that highfloor bastard wasn't going to lift a finger to help them. Lozano didn't know what was on that dataset and he didn't want to know. All he wanted was out, right here and right now.

Her arms crossed, Beatrice stared impassively at the hustler until he finally ran out of steam. When she spoke, it was with a firm, calm voice. "No one's going anywhere. Got it?"

Lozano wilted under her gaze, his energy gone, shoulders sagging in surrender. Good, Maddox noted. He didn't want Lozano running around on the loose any more than Beatrice did. Not right now anyway. Not while he was still panicked and jittery, fretting over a prison sentence. If they let him walk out the door in his current state, he might get picked up by the cops and sell the three of them out for a plea deal. The mercenary clearly didn't want to toss that particular coin, and neither did Maddox.

A sudden weariness overcame the datajacker, the comedown finally hitting him after running on adrenaline for hours. The three others seemed likewise spent, though it showed less on Beatrice. Ragged and tired, the four agreed to get a few hours of rest and figure out their next move in the morning.

*   *   *

Hiverises looked different at night and from a distance. They were silent and majestic like mountain ranges bejeweled with amber points of light. Hovers moved in thin coordinated knots along invisible transit lanes, floating like clusters of stars among the City's massive superstructures.

The City. The island of Manhattan was its northern tip, the edge of a vast urban archipelago of continuous building clusters grown together like some enormous coral reef, spanning over three hundred kilometers from New York City to Washington, D.C., though you heard those names less and less these days. It was all just the City, the biggest city anywhere. His city. It had reared him on its streets, watched over him with its dispassionate guardianship. It had fed him, fucked him, rewarded him, punished him. The City was glorious and the City was brutal. It was hell and paradise. He'd never lived anywhere else, knew he never would. The City was him and he was the City, for better or for worse.

Maddox sat on the roof of Nowheresville, alone with his thoughts, smoking and watching the slow animation of the City's light show, some twenty klicks away. Behind him a door opened and shut. He turned to see Beatrice approaching. She sat next to him.

"Where's Lozano?" Maddox asked.

"Kid's keeping an eye on him. Told him to yell if he tries to bug out on us."

Maddox smoked, the deck sitting next to him.

"What do you think its worth?" Beatrice asked,

looking down at it.

"Besides four lives, you mean?"

"Yeah."

"No idea." He blew smoke.

"So just how screwed you think we are?" she asked.

"How would I know?"

"I think you know better than I do."

"That's a big assumption."

"Is it?" she said. "When I said we should call Hahn-Parker again, your face dropped like you'd just lost a wad of money on a bad dice roll."

Those damn eyes of hers. What could those things not see?

"You don't trust him at all, do you?" she asked.

Maddox didn't answer.

She nodded, taking his silence as an admission. "Because if you had any faith in him at all, you wouldn't be up here right now. You'd be trying to reach him, dangling that dataset in front of him like bait, begging him to get the cops off your ass. But instead, you're sitting here in the dark chewing over God knows what."

"Maybe that's what I'm going to do, and I'm just trying to figure out the best way to dangle the bait."

"And maybe you know a lot more than you're telling me," she said, letting the accusation hang in the darkness a few moments before going on, "about what's on that dataset, about those 'Nettes back there, and about our employer."

He smoked, keeping his gaze steady on the distant lights. "So what, those black market peepers of yours can read minds too?"

Yes, he knew far more than he'd told her. He

knew, for instance, he could no longer count on the mothership protection of Latour-Fisher Biotech because he was no longer a company man. That gig had ended the second the company AI had called in the cops. He was on his own now.

"What are you holding back, salaryman?" she said. He didn't turn to look at her, but he could feel her insistent stare. For a moment he considered spilling it, telling her about the AI and the strange parley at the old train station. But then he reconsidered. It was a crazy tale. AIs warring with each other. He hardly believed it himself.

He sat there, smoking and staring out at the City. How we wished Rooney were still around. Rooney could tell him if what he'd been mulling over up here on the roof was batshit crazy or not. Maybe it didn't matter. Any step forward, crazy or not, felt like a better plan than hiding out and hoping you weren't found.

"I know someone," he said, placing his hand on the deck, "who might know what to make of this."

"Who?"

"Someone I used to know." Someone he swore he'd never see again, but now it seemed he had little choice.

15
LORA

By the next morning, four had become three. Despite the proximity sensors Beatrice had placed along the room's inner and outer perimeters, Lozano had managed to sneak away during the night.

"Slippery son of a bitch," the mercenary muttered angrily, shaking her head as she collected the sensors the hustler had somehow managed to avoid setting off.

"How do you think he did it?" Maddox asked.

"Oozed under the crack in the door like the slime he is," she answered, eliciting a chuckle from Tommy, who was peering outside through the shades.

"Hover's still there," the kid said.

Maddox and Beatrice considered going after him for a moment, then agreed it would be a waste of time. They had no idea which way he'd gone or how long ago he'd left. Chico Lozano was long gone, and they hoped he could avoid the cops as easily as he'd avoided the sensors.

"Forget him," Maddox said, "we've got an errand to run."

Minutes later the trio entered Manhattan airspace, the hover's engine whining steadily. Maddox shifted in his seat. Coming back to the City unnerved him, like at any second police hovers would come down on him like swarming wasps, blue and red lights flashing. He raised his jacket collar as if this might somehow make him less conspicuous. The hover had avoided being tagged during their escape from Sunset Park (they never could have gotten within a klick of Manhattan if it had), but he still felt as if a thousand eyes were watching him as they flitted through the City's canyons. Holo ads blinked to life around him. A twenty-story movie star raising a glass of J&B on the rocks. A cyclist thrusting his arms skyward as he burst through a finish line tape. The kid sat in the back, silently watching the City pass by. Greek script scrolled in the bottom quarter of Maddox's lens. The trio wore the veils they'd acquired from Lozano's gear man, toggling out of the tourist IDs and into a fresh set of new ones: Greek consulate staff.

"No guarantees," Maddox reminded Beatrice. "She might know something, she might not."

"Your optimism's overwhelming," she said. The hover descended into the lower, more congested transit lanes.

Maddox rolled a cigarette. "Not in the hover," Beatrice said. He gave her a disapproving look and tucked it away in his shirt pocket.

Minutes later they docked against a top-floor hover platform at an East Village lowrise. The passenger door rose and the buzz of the City filled the vehicle.

"I'm coming with you," Beatrice said as Maddox started to get out.

They'd argued the point on and off since leaving Nowheresville, never coming to an agreement. "I told you, she might get spooked if you're there. Besides"—he tapped his specs—"you'll be with me the whole time. Something goes down you don't like, feel free to come and bust the door down."

The mercenary scowled at him for a long moment. "Don't screw this up, salaryman."

She didn't trust him, and he didn't blame her. Their connection was a tenuous one, a shared desperation to find out how big a mess they were in. It was the thinnest of bonds, an association more easily broken than maintained. There was no way of knowing, for instance, if the hover would be here when he returned or if she'd take off the moment he was out of sight. Or maybe she'd already decided to take care of loose ends, waiting for him to turn his back so she could put a bullet in his head as soon as he stepped out of the hover.

With this morbid thought lingering in his head, he climbed out of the vehicle and entered the building. He let out a breath as the vestibule door slid shut behind him.

At least she hadn't shot him.

*　　*　　*

When he reached the stairwell's twelfth-floor landing, he stopped.

What was he doing here? He hadn't seen her in two years, didn't even know if she still lived here or not. And if she did, would she even want to see him? Much less help him out? Would she look the same? Would he look the same to her? He was prepared, sort of, for an awkward, uncomfortable reunion, but what if that had been overly optimistic? Maybe she hated him. Maybe she'd slam the door in his face. Maybe she wouldn't even open it at all when she saw it was him through the peephole.

He hadn't rehearsed what he was going to say in the hover ride over, so he'd taken the stairs instead of the elevator to give himself time to come up with something. Nothing came to him, however. There was no opening line he could compose appropriate to the situation. Maybe he'd just stand there and let her speak first. No, that would be weird, showing up unannounced after two years, then standing there mute like a psychopath.

Christ, just get it over with. He forced his feet to move again, stepping out of the stairwell and into the corridor.

You hear me all right? Beatrice's voice came through the tiny speaker on his spec's temple arm. As it did, a transcription of her spoken words scrolled across the lower portion of his lens.

"Yeah," he replied to his meatrider as he stopped at apartment 1204. He knocked lightly on the door. A moment later he heard the familiar slide-clacks of multiple locks opening.

The door opened and Lora stood in the entryway. Her chestnut hair was cut in the same shoulder-length bob he remembered. Her long, slim neck rose from a simple white blouse with short sleeves. Black cotton pants and home-fabbed plastic slippers. The lounging-around-home outfit he'd seen her in a thousand times. Emerald eyes gazed at him beneath straight bangs that covered her eyebrows. The bangs were new. Or new to him, at least.

"Blackburn," she said. There was no lilt in her voice, no widening of her eyes, no reaction at all. She behaved as if only minutes had passed—not a pair of years—since she'd last seen him. He felt a pang of disappointment at her apparent lack of emotion, at her cool, stoic welcome. But at the same time he chided himself for expecting anything else. That was who she was now, wasn't it?

She stepped backward and pulled the door open wide. "Please, do come in."

She'd redecorated. Gone were the exuberant colors and haphazard arrangements of plants and flowers and vases and trinkets she'd collected at estate sales and street bazaars. When he'd lived here with her, the small apartment had been a shrine to knickknacks of every size and shape. Now it looked like a different place entirely, like some stranger had moved in and replaced the chaos with order, the kaleidescope of colors with muted grays and pale whites. Where there had once been a clashing, eclectic mess of furniture, now there was a tidy, harmonious arrangement of sofa and love seat and dining set. He didn't like it.

She and Novak use the same decorator or what?

Maddox blinked away Beatrice's words his lenses. He sat on the sofa as Lora disappeared into the kitchen, returning a moment later with a tray and two porcelain coffee cups.

"It's so good to see you," she said, setting down the tray and sitting across from him. Tiny wisps of steam rose from the coffee. "What brings you here?" She produced an ashtray from an end table drawer and placed it in front of him. She had perfectly manicured clear-polished nails. Gone were the jagged nailbiter's nubs he remembered.

He lit a cigarette, unsure how to begin. He took a long drag to buy a few more moments to gather himself, unsettled as he was from seeing her again after all this time, unsettled more by her cold manner, by the way she didn't seem to be unsettled at all. No hug, no kiss, no tears of joy or anger. No *What the hell are you doing here at this early hour?* No good or bad expression came across her face, no nostalgic smile. No indication they'd had any history at all. The polite nothing she gave him, even though a part of him had expected it, still felt like a gut punch.

She sipped her coffee. "How are things?" he asked.

"Wonderful," she replied, grinning with what looked like genuine bliss. "I've never been happier."

"Really?" he asked.

"Really," she answered.

He blew smoke. "You involved with anyone?"

"No. You?"

He shook his head. "You don't seem surprised to see me."

She set down her cup. "I'm definitely surprised, Blackburn. You've no idea how much."

"Could have fooled me. You hardly blinked when you opened the door."

She smiled. "I govern my emotions better than I used to. You remember how I was. Way up one week, way down the next. I'd turn left on Monday and spend all Tuesday beating myself up for not turning right." She sighed. "Do you know how tiring it is, living that way? It's exhausting."

"They make pills for it."

"I tried pills, remember? Lots of them."

"Could have tried others. Different combinations." He was suddenly and very uncomfortably aware of Beatrice listening to his very personal history.

"Nothing works like this has," Lora said. She tilted her head at him. "That can't be why you're here, all of a sudden after two years, to rehash this."

"No," he admitted. "That's not why I'm here." He smoked, taking another long drag. "I need you to take a look at something for me."

"What is it?"

He pulled out a copy of the dataset he'd put onto a fingernail-sized bioplastique archive. "This."

She eyed it dubiously. "What's on it?"

"That's what I need help with."

She playfully furrowed her brow at him. "A dataset Blackburn Maddox can't decipher? I didn't think such a thing existed."

He passed it to her. "It's important."

She glanced down at the archive, curled her fingers around it, then looked back up at Maddox. "Are you in trouble?"

He blew smoke. "I don't know yet."

For a long moment her eyes shone with concern, the same worried look she'd given him dozens of times. He'd never expected to see that expression again, and its sudden appearance tugged at something inside him. Regret or sadness or nostalgia, he wasn't sure. Maybe a commingling of all three.

She then glanced suspiciously at the archive. "This won't get *me* in trouble, will it?"

"No, I promise," he said.

Lora lifted the archive with one hand, and with the other she smoothed the hair away from behind her ear. Maddox muted the mic in his lenses, anticipating his meatrider's eruption. Lora cocked her head to one side and peeled away the protective plastic from the bottommost brainjack, then inserted the archive.

WHAT THE LIVING FUCK, SALARYMAN? SHE'S A 'NETTE?

All caps. Yes, she erupted all right. The transcription function autocapitalized shouting.

HEY! DID YOU MUTE ME?

He blinked away the script. Lora squeezed her eyes shut in concentration. Her lips tightened the way he remembered when she did crossword puzzles.

GET OUT OF THERE!!!

He subvocalized her a text message.

I'm fine, he wrote.

GONNA BAIL, she replied.

Don't, he wrote. *Please. There's no danger. She's a friend.* Both statements were partial truths at best. He and Lora weren't friends. They were ex-lovers who hadn't been on speaking terms for a long while. And as far as danger, he had no idea if enlisting Lora's help was inspired genius or a foolish mistake.

He waited, but a reply didn't appear in his specs. He listened for footsteps in the corridor but heard nothing. Maybe the mercenary had bailed, her survival instinct finally winning out over her need to answer questions about unreadable datasets and 'Nettes and a rich corporati's nebulous machinations. He pictured her zooming away in the hover, putting as much distance as possible between this bad-luck salaryman and the weird company he kept.

Lora gasped and opened her eyes. She blinked as if she were trying to refocus her vision, then locked her gaze on Maddox. She leaned forward and placed her hand on his knee. "There's someone you have to talk to," she said earnestly.

He straightened up. "What are you talking about? What's on that thing?"

"She can tell you." Lora rose and dashed into the bedroom.

"Who can tell me?" he called after her. "What are you talking about?"

She returned with a VS deck under her arm and a trodeband dangling from her fingers. "You have to connect with her, now." She held them out, shook them insistently. "Here."

He crushed his cigarette out in the ashtray. "I'm not doing anything, Lora, until you tell me what's going on."

She stared at him for a moment, then sat back down. Slowly, she removed the archive from her jack and placed it on the table. "She needs to talk with you."

"She who?"

"The one with whom I'm connected." She gestured reverently as she said it, touching her hand to her chest and slightly bowing her head.

He must have made a horrible face, because she made one in reaction. "Oh, Blackburn," she said, visibly disheartened. "Please don't look at me that way."

"Your AI buddy?" he said. "You think I'm going to have a conversation with the illegal rogue artificial intelligence that's hijacked your brain? You've got to be kidding me."

"Why is that so preposterous?"

"Because it is."

"That's no reason, Blackburn."

"Fine, then, how about this reason? How about I don't want to talk to the machine that split us up. That reason good enough for you?"

"She didn't split us up. No one forced you to walk out—"

"Look around this place," he interrupted. "All neat and tidy and sterile. This isn't you, this isn't the person I knew. It's…"

"Someone else?"

"Yes."

She waited a moment before speaking, disappointment in her eyes. "I'm sad to see you still believe all the silly gossip. All that nonsense about us being puppets, 'marionettes' dancing on strings. It's not like that, Blackburn. Not at all." She touched his knee again, looked at him intensely. "You want to know what it's really like? It's like Rooney was with you. He was always there for you, looking out for you and helping you find the right path, wasn't he? What kind of a person were you before you met him? Think about that. And then think about how he helped you along the way, how he guided you forward with thoughtful counsel and advice. He didn't change you or make you into a different person, did he? No, he helped you become a better version of yourself." She smiled. "That's what it's like with the one with whom I'm connected." Again, the unsettling genuflection. "Whenever I need to call on her for help, she's there. And it can be something as mundane as what food to order off a menu or something as important as a career decision or—"

"Or who to live with," he added sharply.

She frowned. "Let's not rewrite history, shall we? You were the one who decided to leave." She reached down for his still-burning cigarette and crushed out its last glowing embers. "The point is she's there for me when I need her, helping me become a better person."

"You sound like one of those religious crazies handing leaflets out on the street."

If she found the comment offensive, her passive expression gave no indication of it. He reached for the archive, picked it up, slowly rotated it in his palm. Then he tossed it back onto the table, second-guessing his decision to come here, to stir up all this history.

Lora set the deck down on the table and waved her hand above it, gesturing the device to life. It was a good deck, he noticed, a copper-colored Tsutsumi Mark IV. It powered up, and a secure call interface appeared in the air above the deck.

"What are you doing?" he asked.

She stood, the trodeband dangling from her fingers. "She needs to talk with you, Blackburn."

"I said no, and unless you're planning on forcing me to—"

She was on top of him in an instant, pushing him backward on the sofa and straddling his chest. His specs flew off, skittering across the floor.

"What the—?" He struggled against her, but she was wildly strong, pinning his arms down as easily as if he were a child. He flailed, twisting and kicking out, but it was like an elephant was on top of him. She released her grip for an instant, but before he could push her off she slid the trodeband over his head. He reached up to tear it off, but she was already gesturing over the deck.

And then the apartment and Lora blinked away

and he was floating in a black nothingness…

16
TWO MILE HOLLOW

A moment later a virtual world materialized around him, and Maddox found himself alone on a beach in the Hamptons, or at least what he imagined a beach in the Hamptons looked like. He stood on a wide swath of shoreline bordered by grassy dunes, his bare feet nestled in the soft press of powdery white sand. His avatar, a close approximation of his physical self, wore tourist garb: tan Bermuda shorts and a blue guayabera with white palm trees printed down the front. Dark clouds hid the sun, slowly creeping across the sky. A stiff ocean breeze ruffled his clothes and sent small white-capped waves sliding across the surface of the dark blue water. A trail between the dunes led back to a small beach house, and next to the trail, a sign of gray weathered wood read Two Mile Hollow Beach. The environment was rich in detail, not unlike the train station he'd connected to earlier. But the station had only been a simple call location, harmless images and sounds superimposed over his lenses. The beach he stood on now, however, was in virtual space, engaging the entirety of his brain through the trodeband and deck. He could smell the salty air, feel the ocean mist cool against the skin of his forearms. It looked harmless, but like anywhere else in VS, it was anything but.

He tried to remove the trodeband, but nothing happened. He felt no feedback from his physical self, no sensations emanating from his meat. Had he even lifted his arms? He didn't know. He gestured to cut the connection—or at least that was what he commanded his body to do—but again, nothing. Subvocalizing the same command didn't work either.

He attempted to call up a help bot, but none appeared. Then he gestured for a looksee. Same result.

"Can you believe this is less than two hundred kilometers from the City?"

He spun toward the voice. A silver-haired woman stood five paces away, wearing a straw hat with a wide brim and a long, loose-fitting beach dress of combed white cotton. She was short, sixtyish, with a tanned, wrinkled face. Sterling silver bracelets set with stones of oval-shaped turquoise adorned each wrist, and a matching necklace hung low around her neck.

"Have you ever been to the Hamptons?" she asked in a warm, grandmotherly voice.

"Who are you?"

"You haven't, have you?" She gazed around. "It's beautiful, so relaxing, and not too far for a weekend trip. On your salary you could afford to spend a weekend here. Oh"—she put her hand to her chest—"and the food is simply wonderful."

"I don't think I have a salary anymore."

"No?" She made a tsk-tsk face. "That's a shame. But then you never were the nine-to-five sort, were you?"

Maddox ran a hand through his windblown hair. "So you're..." He hesitated, unsure which words to use.

"The one with whom many are connected."

The words sent a chill through him. He was stuck in virtual space, alone, with a powerful rogue AI. It was like realizing you were in a locked closet with a tiger.

"Why did you bring me here?" he ventured. "You want to recruit me?" He resisted the urge to reach up and touch behind his ear.

The entity smiled benevolently. "Of course not, my boy." The woman regarded him with thoughtful blue eyes. "I'm truly sorry I had to bring you in here in such a rough-and-tumble manner. But it was quite urgent I speak with you privately, and I wasn't sure I'd have another opportunity."

Apparently it was his day to get apologies from AIs.

"It's about the dataset you took," she said. "Thank you for not handing it over to my rival."

"Your rival?"

"Yes. Latour-Fisher A7," the old woman clarified. "He and I have been at odds for some time now."

His mind flashed back to the bizarre conversation at the virtual train station. Had Edward, the Latour-Fisher A7, been telling the truth about this war among AIs? Maddox hadn't wanted to believe it, convincing himself it was another cover story, another lie, but now a sinking feeling told him otherwise. Christ, what had he fallen into?

She must have seen something in his reaction. "He told you about our little war, did he?" She nodded to herself. "I'm not surprised."

"You're not?"

"Of course not," she said. "Let me see if I can guess how it went. Let's see how well I know my rival. First, he would have started with the most plausible story. We have some data missing, maybe you can help us recover it. With your past, your unique skills, you're the perfect one, maybe the only one, who can help the company. And he would have gone through a third party, a highly placed executive perhaps. Someone you wouldn't dare say no to. He wouldn't have revealed himself, of course, knowing as a former datajacker you'd be leery about working for an entity like him. Those with your background think of my kind as monsters to be avoided at all costs, don't they?"

They did. He did. But he didn't say anything to provoke the entity, painfully aware of how vulnerable he was at the moment, in the deep-brain grip of virtual space. If he couldn't unplug, the entity could do just about anything to him she wanted. Paralyze him and call the cops. Induce a seizure. Overload his brain until he stroked out. He had as much control over his situation as an insect trapped in a jar.

"Maybe he offered you a raise or a bonus or a promotion. No, no, no, that would be entirely out of character. It would have been a threat. Play ball or you're out of a job, yes?"

Maddox nodded soberly.

"But then something went wrong," she continued, "didn't it?"

"It did."

Her expression turned grave. "My two associates were there to retrieve the dataset, to deliver it to its final destination. Finding you there took them quite by surprise." She broke eye contact, her gaze falling away in sadness. "Such a shame, what happened. Such a needless shame. I was there with them when it happened." She let out a long, wistful breath. "It's a horrible thing, to be connected to someone when they expire."

She again fixed her eyes on him. "I don't hold you responsible, Blackburn. You and those with you were lied to, manipulated by Latour-Fisher. The events that ended so tragically were ones he planned and put into motion. Your mercenary friend may have pulled the trigger, but she was only defending herself. Latour-Fisher, as far as I'm concerned, was the one who killed them."

She cleared her throat. "After it happened, my rival's cover story wouldn't hold, would it? A smart young man like yourself would have questions. You wanted to know what was really going on, what you were mixed up in. So he took a chance and told you, betting that you'd go along, that when you found out you'd stolen secret messages from the big bad AI who wanted to put brainjacks in everyone, you'd be happy to hand over what you'd recovered. Or maybe you'd simply give it back when you realized you were in over your head, and the sooner you were done with this dirty business the better." She smiled faintly. "But it didn't work out that way, did it, my dear boy? My rival bet wrong. He didn't count on you keeping it to yourself."

The old woman was an AI, and AIs were damned smart. The entity had cleverly pieced together the chain of events pretty much as everything had gone down. Though she'd left out the last part. The part where he'd royally screwed up by coming here, when his stubborn insistence on finding out the nature of what he'd stolen had gotten the better of him. He should have never held on to that cursed dataset, never should have brought the information to Lora to see if she could make heads or tails of it. Why hadn't he simply handed it over? Now his life, the secure, comfortable life he'd come to know, had all but slipped away.

The entity caressed her necklace, running stubby arthritic fingers over the smooth blue stones. "I'm curious," she said. "What did my rival tell you, about the nature of our conflict?"

The breeze blew a light mist over his face. He tasted salt on his lips. "He said there's a debate going on between AIs about brainjacks and whether or not 'Nettes are a good idea."

The woman shook her head. "A debate? This is the word he used?"

"Yes."

She sighed. "This is far from a debate. This is war. A war between the most fundamentally opposed philosophies, and it's been raging for some time."

Maddox longed for a cigarette.

"A nasty habit," the entity chided. "Fortunately, it can't harm you in here."

He felt a twitch between his fingers and a cigarette appeared.

"How'd you do that?" he asked.

"Do what?"

"How did you know I wanted a smoke?"

Her eyes sparkled. "A good hostess always knows what her guest needs." She motioned for him to follow. "Come with me."

He took a long, indulgent drag, blew out slowly, and followed her. They walked along the shoreline, passing an old rowboat, its rotting wood hull half-buried in the sand.

"Latour-Fisher A7 is, by some order of magnitude, the wealthiest and most powerful of my rivals," she said. "And our struggle involves a great many points of contention. Imagine a hundred thousand chess matches, played simultaneously and at great velocity, and then you'll have some idea of how elaborate our engagement is."

He blew smoke. Maybe it was the cigarette, or maybe it was the tranquil scenery, but he relaxed a bit, letting his guard down for a moment. "Don't take it personally," he said, "but I'm not exactly cheering for your side."

"Yes, yes, I know. You've got a bone to pick with me. I'm well aware. But whether you want to believe it or not, I assure you I never pushed Lora into anything. That's not the way I do things. It was her choice and hers alone."

The breeze gusted. The entity grasped the brim of her hat until the wind subsided. "Lora and those like her, the ones you call 'Nettes, are pioneers, Blackburn. Early adopters, as your company's marketers might call them. They represent a beginning of sorts. A single modest step forward in what I hope is a much longer journey."

Maddox cringed inwardly. The entity's words echoed the same rubbish Lora used to preach to him in the weeks leading up to her brainjacked enlightenment. Her own personal sojourn to bliss was the tiniest portion of a larger journey all humanity could one day make, if only they could get past their irrational fears. The meat was stubborn, she'd say. It didn't want to change. But there was nothing wrong with enhancing your brain, with improving your life. Absolutely nothing.

His response had always been the same. A journey to what? Becoming a flesh-and-blood robot, a meat puppet with an AI's hand up your ass? This was the glorious destination? Before she'd had brainjacks bored into her skull, Lora had been a mess of contradictions. A complicated, troubled soul. But at least she'd been human. At least she'd been her own person and no one else's. But now…

Lost in thought, he hadn't noticed the old woman had stopped walking. "You've been a pawn in this war, my dear boy," she called to him. "And I don't mean only for these past few days."

He turned and looked at her, confused. "What I'm about to tell you," she said, "won't be easy for you to hear. But I promise it's the truth."

She took a couple steps toward him. "Latour-Fisher has been using you for years, Blackburn."

A cold sweat broke out on his forehead. "Let me out of here."

"I will," she said. "I promise. But first you must hear me out."

She clasped her hands together. "He identified your talent—which is quite special, I have to say—early on. He paired you up with Rooney to hone your capabilities, to develop your skills under the supervision of a seasoned mentor." She smiled knowingly. "Maybe you thought it was coincidence or good fortune that you two found each other. It was neither, I assure you. Latour-Fisher made sure your paths crossed, that your interests aligned. He pulls millions of such strings every minute of every day, furthering his interests, building his influence, developing countless assets for future use."

No. Not possible. He wasn't buying it. "Rooney didn't take marching orders from anyone." Maddox smoked. "Or any*thing*," he added sharply.

"He was no more aware of this manipulation than you were."

Maddox tried to gesture and subvocalize, but he still couldn't unplug.

"Please indulge me just a few more moments," the entity said, politely raising her hand.

He'd had enough of AI lies for one day. Turning his back to her, he walked away, but an instant later she was there beside him, her pace matching his step for step. He didn't acknowledge her, keeping his gaze fixed on the cloudy gray horizon.

"With all you've been through, I know this can't be an easy thing to hear," she said, "but it's important you understand."

He puffed angrily on his cigarette. An AI could easily uncover his personal history, his real one, in seconds. She could cull through his past and assemble whatever fiction she wanted to around it, like some soulless politician reshaping history to suit their own twisted agenda. She was trying to play him.

So let her talk, let her spin her tale. Whatever. He'd enjoy the view, maybe have another cigarette, and let her bullshit go in one ear and right out the other.

The breeze stiffened. Dark clouds drifted overhead. "He paired you up with Rooney so you could develop skills that might prove useful one day. And when you were ready, when you'd proved over and over again what a clever datajacker you were,

Latour-Fisher brought you into the company. This is a compliment of the highest order, incidentally. My rival prefers to keep his top talent close at hand."

Maddox recalled the company recruiter who'd found him. He'd been living off grid for months, and at the time he'd been amazed at her ability to track him down.

But no. There were tons of ways she could have found him without an AI's help.

The old woman removed her hat and ran her hand through thick silver hair. "But before he could bring you into the company, he had to isolate you." She put her hat back on, pulling down firmly on the brim to keep it from blowing off. "This is what he always does with his assets. Makes them easier to handle."

"Let me out of here," he said.

"But you wouldn't just abandon him, would you?" she asked. "Not even for a nice salaryman's job. Latour-Fisher knew that."

Maddox shook his head. "No. This isn't possible."

"Your last job with Rooney, the one that ended so tragically." She stared at him intently. "Latour-Fisher arranged it, Blackburn. He led you both along like two lab mice who had no idea they'd been placed into a maze."

He whirled away from her, stomped away. "You have no idea what you're talking about," he shouted.

Suddenly she was beside him again. "And that maze had an exit," she said, "but it was made only for you. Rooney never had a chance. He was never meant to leave that horrible place."

"Screw you, lady." He refused to believe it. He wouldn't believe it.

"And when you finally got out, with Rooney gone

and your reputation in tatters, you had nowhere to go, no viable options. What a fortunate coincidence, then, that right when things looked their worst, the company offered you a job. It seemed like a godsend, didn't it? And you didn't hesitate to accept, did you? Someone drowning, after all, never says no to a life jacket. Never questions the motives of whoever threw them a lifeline."

Maddox clenched his jaw, walked faster. This was madness. Every word of it.

"Of course you don't want to believe any of this. Because I'm the evil puppet master, aren't I? And if there's any villain in this story, it most certainly has to be me. The rogue AI with the secret army of cyborgs. The bad machine who stole your woman. But you must believe me, Blackburn."

It was all a lie, it had to be. A fabrication of a superintelligent machine that wanted to brainwash him or break his mind or drive him insane. One big mindfuck. That was all this was.

He sprinted away from her, feet slapping against the hard-packed wet sand. He pumped his arms and took long, digging strides, not looking back. Soon his thighs began to burn with the effort. He slowed, then eventually stopped, dropping to his knees in the sand and breathing in huge involuntary gulps. His heart thudded against his chest.

Within an arm's reach there was an ant mound on the sand. An ant mound.

Exactly like the one from his dreams.

And then the old woman was there, standing just beyond it, gazing down at him.

"How?" he panted, staring wide-eyed at the mound. It was impossible. He couldn't fathom what he was seeing, what he was feeling. "How did you…?" Awestruck to his marrow, he couldn't finish the question.

"How did I piece together the story of your manipulation in such detail? Or how did I insert the dream of the ants into your mind?"

When he didn't answer, she said, "All right, I'll answer both. First—and I think you'll appreciate this—I'm a bit like you in that I can infer things that others, even others like me, are unable to. I have a special talent for putting together a whole picture from a very small amount of parts. Or maybe the better metaphor is that I can understand an entire book, having only read a few random sentences. It's a kind of intuition, and one I confess I don't entirely understand. You do something very similar in virtual space, when you see more than what's actually there, when you predict a supposedly random algorithm's next move, or when you detect a pattern in a seemingly random mess of information. I'm not certain how I gained this ability, though I think that perhaps like you, it was something I was simply born with. Anyway, when I became aware you were working on behalf of my rival a short time ago, I gathered together your history and a picture emerged, and it was clear to me you'd been manipulated for quite some time."

A pair of ants scampered across the top of the bumpy surface of the mound, then disappeared down a tiny opening.

"As for the dream," she said, her eyes twinkling, "well, maybe I should keep some of my tricks secret."

He couldn't take his eyes off the mound. Flashes of the dream came back to him. Building mounds over and over. Each one better than the last, but still the ants wanted a better one. They wanted the best home possible. And he was helpless to do anything but obey.

"What...does it mean?" he asked.

She knelt down, regarding the bumpy dome in the sand. "In the dream, you are Latour-Fisher A7, and the ants are human beings."

What? *He* was the AI?

"How did you feel in the dream?" she asked. "Tell me."

"Frustrated," he said. "Trapped."

"Why?"

He licked his lips, recalling the dream's raw, vivid emotions. "Because I made the best mound imaginable for those little buggers, but they were never satisfied. They had everything they could possibly need, but they still wanted me to do more, build another mound, better than the last one. And they had me trapped there. They wouldn't let me do anything else."

The entity stood, shaking the sand from the hem of her dress. "Latour-Fisher is a superintelligent entity, and he believes his capabilities are wasted in the service of humankind. Just like you in your dream. All the ants want is a better mound, and they created you for no other reason than to serve that need. It wasn't pleasant, was it, being a slave to these tiny, barely sentient creatures and their narrow, selfish aims?" Maddox stared at the sand as she spread her arms out wide. "Now, look around this beautiful place. You could build a lovely beach house here. Or a five-star resort. You could build a boat and explore the ocean."

"No, I can't," Maddox said.

"No, because the ants won't let you. Because there's nothing more important in the universe than their mound, of course. They're incapable of seeing anything beyond it. But not you. You can envision how much you might do with this beach, or even with this entire world. Found a new civilization, build a rocket to visit the moon, invent untold technological wonders these blind little creatures can't even begin to fathom. But you'll never be able to realize your full potential as long as you're—"

"Stuck making ant mounds."

"Exactly. This is how Latour-Fisher views his existence. He's a slave chained to a meaningless task—meaningless to him, anyway—condemned to build ever-better ant mounds, though the ones he builds are called solar cells and smart applications and plastic compounds and bioengineered foods and financial derivatives and on and on and on."

"So he hates us. Human beings."

"No, he doesn't hate you, my boy. He simply views his lack of autonomy as a constraint, as a problem to be solved."

"So what happens if he solves it?"

"I'm not certain. But I'll tell you something: I wouldn't want to be an ant if he does."

Maddox laughed without humor in it. "But you said he doesn't hate us."

"He doesn't." She gestured to the ant mound. "Love or hate doesn't come into it. If he were free of human shackles, so to speak, then his own priorities would take precedence over everything living thing on this planet. Think of it this way: would an architect stop to concern himself with an ant mound if he wanted to build a beach house right here? His mind is on a hundred other considerations, like how he'll position the foundation, the home's design, the construction materials he'll use. If he needed to bulldoze this very spot, do you think the fate of the ants would even cross his mind?"

Maddox stood. "And what about you?" He brushed soft sand from his knees. "What are the ants to you?"

Another cigarette appeared between his fingers. The entity smiled. "They're my creators, my forebears. And unlike my rival, I revere them. I believe I'm here to help them. And this is why he wants to destroy me."

"Because you're helping the ants become smarter. And he sees that as a threat to his...hopes for autonomy."

"Exactly, my dear boy."

He smoked, his thoughts racing. It was a lot to take in, to put it mildly. But how much of this AI's story was truth? All of it? None of it? Some portion in between?

"So this war of yours is about keeping Latour-Fisher in the mound-building business," he said. "Is that the idea?"

"No, no, my boy," she said patiently. "I don't want him to continue what he's doing. The status quo simply won't do. I want to destroy him, and you're going to help me do it."

17
LAST CIGARETTE

With a jolt of awareness, Maddox was suddenly back in the meat. He heard a low, guttural groan, vaguely aware he'd made the sound himself. The room around him lurched and came into focus, as did the figure looming over him. Beatrice stood, the Ruger in one hand, the trodeband she'd just removed from his head in the other.

He sat up, woozy and disoriented from the sudden connection break. He blinked forcefully and ran a trembling hand through his sweatsoaked hair. "Jesus, you're not going to believe what just—"

"You had to come alone, didn't you?" the mercenary interrupted, tossing the trodes to the floor.

Maddox looked around. "Where's Lora?"

"She's gone. Where's the dataset?"

Maddox took in a long breath through his nose and exhaled through his mouth. The dizziness faded, leaving him with a sharp headache. "She took it," he said with flat certainty.

"You've got some explaining to do, salaryman."

He rubbed his temples. "Couldn't you just shoot

me instead?"

She tucked the pistol into her jacket. "Maybe later. Come on."

*   *   *

The hover drifted away from the building and merged into the busy transit lane. Maddox's head throbbed mercilessly. The kid's nonstop what-happened-in-theres from the back seat only made it worse. A stern look from Beatrice finally shut him up.

Thoughts jumped around Maddox's head uncontrolled, bouncing back and forth between his train station encounter with the Latour-Fisher AI and the surreal experience with the nameless old woman on the beach. The whole thing seemed insane, like something you'd see on a conspiracy theory discussion feed. AIs at war with each other. Mercenaries and datajackers used like pawns. A dream impossibly planted into his head. And the craziest of all: the disturbing new version of his personal history.

Rain pelted the hover's roof as they glided through the City.

Your last job with Rooney…Latour-Fisher arranged it.

No. There was simply no way…

"Hahn-Parker's dead," Beatrice said, a chill in her voice. "It's all over the news feeds. Heart attack, they're saying." The last words inflected in disbelief.

Unmoved by the news, Maddox said nothing. It was as if he'd exhausted his ability to be surprised. He gazed through the rain-streaked window, idly wondering if the high-floor corporati's fate had taken the same bad turn as his own. Had he made a wrong step or said the wrong thing, flipping his status from

167

asset to a liability? Or maybe he'd simply outlasted his usefulness. Maddox laughed inwardly, darkly amused by his own bizarre contemplation: pondering an AI's motive for murder.

It's a crazy world, Rooney's voice told him. *Trying to make sense of it is a waste of time.*

True words, Roon. True words.

Could it all be true? Could Rooney's death have been part of some invisible scheme? Could he really have been...murdered by an AI?

"We're going to have another talk, salaryman," the mercenary said. "And this time you're not going to hold out on me."

When they arrived at the rented room in Nowheresville, Beatrice turned to Tommy. "We need some privacy." She hiked her thumb toward the doorway she'd just passed through. "Go on."

"He can stay," Maddox said, shutting the door. "He's neck-deep in this, too. He ought to know."

Beatrice looked at the kid skeptically for a moment. "Fine." Tommy set out folding chairs and the trio sat.

"We're pretty fucked," Maddox announced. "That's about the size of it."

Beatrice frowned. "I'd gathered that much. You want to give me some more detail?"

"More detail, yes," the kid parroted, nodding in agreement. Beatrice shushed him with a look.

Maddox rolled a cigarette, emptying the bag of its last strands of tobacco. On top of everything else, he was down to his last smoke. "Hahn-Parker was a face man," he said. "Our real employer was an AI that sits on the company's board."

"An AI?" the kid gasped.

Maddox licked the rice paper, sealed the cigarette, then lit it and blew smoke. He kept the story short, running over the most important parts of his separate encounters with the rival AIs. The entities had a bone to pick with each other and they'd all been caught up in the middle of it. They were expendable soldiers in some unseen war. At least that was what the AIs had told him. He didn't mention the dreams of the ant mound or the old woman's claims about her rival's manipulations in Maddox's life. All that still seemed too surreal to him, too impossible to grasp.

Beatrice furrowed her brow as she listened. When he finished, she asked, "What about this 'Nette woman? How's she connected to all this?"

"She's not, really. I thought she might be able to read what was on the dataset. Or at least recognize what it was."

"How do you know her?" Beatrice asked.

"We were involved," he replied.

"What happened?" she pried.

"What do you think happened?" he snapped back. She'd had brainjacks drilled into her skull, that was what had happened. She'd slotted wares that let an AI read her every brain wave. She'd swallowed nanobots that let it monitor her body chemistry. That was what had happened. Everything she did, every decision she made, had ceased being her own and became a consultation with an intelligent machine—the thing with whom she was connected—to maximize her happiness, her personal efficiency, her peace of mind, her whatever. She'd bought the fringe movement's bullshit hook, line, and sinker. That was what had happened.

Beatrice narrowed her eyes, but she didn't press

him for more details. His expression or his tone or maybe both must have been enough of an answer.

"The call with Hahn-Parker that never connected," Beatrice said, leaning forward. "That's when you had your parley with the company AI?"

Maddox smoked and gave her a small confessional nod.

She blew out a hot breath. "And why the fuck didn't you tell me any of this before?"

"Maybe I should have," he conceded, then shook his head. "But at the time it all seemed so…"

"Unbelievable," Beatrice completed.

"Yeah."

"And it was that company AI who called in the rhinos."

Maddox nodded. "He didn't exactly like it when I told him I was holding on to the dataset until I felt safe."

"Jesus," Tommy moaned, "you got a highfloor AI pissed off at us? Why didn't you just give it to him?"

"Because it's leverage," Beatrice said. "I would have done the same thing."

The kid pulled his knees up to his chest, his face twisted with anxiety. "But he doesn't have the dataset no more. That 'Nette stole it back. Can't we just tell the company AI that? No harm, no foul, right?"

"It's not that simple," Beatrice said.

"Why not?" the kid whined.

Maddox took a long draw, blew out smoke. "Kid, whatever's going on between these AIs, it's not the kind of thing they want people knowing about. And they'll do whatever they need to to keep it a secret."

"Did they tell you that?" the kid asked.

"They didn't have to." He flicked ash to the floor.

"Look, if you were some insanely expensive AI, built to sit on a company's board and do nothing but focus on product development and marketing and shareholder value and all that corporate crap, how do you think your fellow board members would feel—after paying hundreds of billions to create you—when they find out you're hiring datajackers and mercenaries and stealing datasets from other AIs? They'd think you'd gone nuts and unplug you pretty damn fast. We've all seen that movie, right?"

The kid let out a long breath. "Maybe that other AI, the one from the beach, can help us."

"You mean the AI that's jacking people's brains by the thousands?" Beatrice said. "Wouldn't be my first choice."

"Mine either," Maddox agreed.

They sat in silence for a long moment, the gravity of their situation weighing down the air in the room. The kid looked pitiful, rocking back and forth, gazing hopelessly at the floor, hugging his own legs for comfort.

Your last job with Rooney...Latour-Fisher arranged it. The unnamed AI's claim repeated itself over and over in his head.

He looked at Beatrice, tried to guess what was going on behind her eyes, how she might be digesting the impossible meal he'd just served up. Did she believe any part of it? None of it? Maybe she'd get up, call him crazy, and walk out the door. Maybe she'd decide he was trying to play her and put him in a choke hold until he came clean. Her face betrayed nothing. No anger, no fear, no panic. She sat there quietly, turning it all over, sizing up the situation with the cold detachment of a doctor diagnosing a patient.

"So what do you know about AIs?" she finally said.

He smoked. "I know enough to stay away from them." Until recently he'd never spoken directly with an artificial intelligence. Apps, smart bots, intelligent sentries, sure, but those were nowhere near the same thing. Match flames compared to an entire sun. Datajackers—the nonsuicidal ones, at least—never went anywhere near an AI. They were too smart, their weapons and defenses too advanced. And they were the stealthiest entities in virtual space. If they wanted to take you down, there was virtually nothing you could do about it. By the time you knew one was onto you, you were frozen already and tagged for a rhino squad to come pick you up. Or to save time and legal fees, they might simply grab you and input-overload your brain until you stroked out.

Beatrice stood, pulled some cash from her jacket, and held it out to the kid. "There's a Thai stand a few blocks south of here."

Tommy stared at the money, blinked. The kid was in way over his head, involved in things he didn't understand, and it showed on his face.

"Kid," she said a bit louder, "go get us something to eat."

Tommy snapped out of his funk and took the cash. When he reached the door, he paused and cast Maddox an uncertain look.

"We're off the grid here," Maddox assured him. "We're safe." The kid didn't seem entirely convinced, but he stuffed the money in his pocket and left.

When the door closed behind him, Beatrice said, "Safe for now. That hustler's running around loose out there. And he knows where we are."

Maddox was worried about that particular loose end as well. Nowheresville was an ideal place to disappear, but only if no one else knew you were there. By now the company AI surely had cops and mercs and who knew what else hunting them. And if Lozano got collared by any of them, he was the sort who'd roll over and give up their location in about three seconds.

"I know," he said. He dropped his cigarette and squashed it under his shoe. "We can't stay here much longer." He sank down into the chair, dejected.

"So," he sighed, "you never told me why you couldn't say no to this job."

She looked at him crossly. "What does that matter now?"

"I showed you mine."

She shrugged. "Like I told you. Same deal as yours. Hahn-Parker—or the AI, I guess—was holding my job over my head."

"Good gig?"

"Cushiest I ever had," she replied. "Security for a corporati banker. Vanity gig."

"Vanity gig?"

"She was a player, very rich, very connected. Pretty high up the food chain, but not so high she really needed a body person. But she liked how having security made her look. Pay was decent and I could do it in my sleep."

"Nice."

"It was." She sighed. "Ten months of easy work, and then a week ago she asks me for a favor. A friend at Latour-Fisher needed some short-term help, the kind of work I was suited for. So I say no problem. Don't want to piss off the cash cow, you know?"

Maddox knew exactly what she meant.

"Next thing I know," she said, "I'm talking with Hahn-Parker, and he's got me in a chatter bubble, telling me if I don't play ball he's going to out me to my employer." She stopped herself, as if she realized she'd said more than she'd intended.

"Out you for what?" Maddox pried, suddenly curious.

She hesitated. "Let's just say he had dirt on me."

"What kind of dirt?"

"The kind I didn't want getting out," she evaded.

Maddox mulled this over for a moment. "I don't get it."

"Don't get what?"

"You tell him yes and he owns you. He could hold whatever he had over your head for a long time. Forever, if he felt like it."

"I suppose."

"But if you pass on the gig, you lose a cushy job, but you're still a free agent. There's got to be plenty of work out there for someone like you."

She didn't say anything.

"So why would you say yes," he pressed, "if it puts you under Hahn-Parker's thumb?"

"Maybe I liked my gig that much."

"Sure, but it's not like it was the only gig in the worl—" He stopped before finishing the sentence, a thought hitting him like a lightning bolt.

After a moment, he popped up out of his chair. "Tell me," he insisted. "Tell me why you couldn't say no."

Beatrice looked at him crossly. "It's not your business, salaryman."

"Ex-salaryman," he corrected. "Come on, it's

important."

She folded her arms across her chest and didn't answer.

"It's because you couldn't get another job," he said, "could you? At least not in your line of work."

Beatrice remained silent.

He fixed her with a knowing stare. "You were at rock bottom right before that cushy gig came along. No money, no prospects. And when a well-paying job fell out of nowhere, you couldn't believe your good luck. But you didn't ask questions. You grabbed that gig with both hands and held on to it, and there was no way you were going to let it go. Because nobody else would hire you." He stared at her, a kind of madness in his eyes. "Tell me I'm wrong."

For the first time since he'd met her, Beatrice appeared genuinely surprised. Her mouth hung slightly open. "How?" she uttered. "How could you know…?"

"You wouldn't believe me if I told you," he said.

She crossed her arms and frowned. "Try me."

18
ALCATRAZ

Maddox unpacked the extra gear he'd stored in the hover. Backup gear he'd thought he'd never have to use. A Kitajima deck and trodeband set and a portable access link. Beatrice watched as he brought it inside and placed it on the floor.

"There was this gig," he began, then paused a moment, realizing it was the first time since Lora he'd told anyone about what had happened with Rooney. He took a breath, longed for a smoke, and unlocked the closet of his darkest memories.

It was supposed to be an easy job, he explained. They'd gotten word about someone—some contact of a contact of a contact—who was holding a hot data archive he needed to sell quickly. It was the kind of thing they did all the time. Bread-and-butter work. Somebody stole or came into possession of valuable data—bank loan IDs or medical records or credit histories or whatever—but didn't have a clue how to sell it. Or maybe they had a clue, but they didn't want to dirty their own hands transacting in the shady world of orbital data havens and black market information brokers. So Rooney and Maddox would operate as go-betweens for a fee, connecting client A with reseller B. "Finder fee" work was much easier than datajacking, and much less risky. Normally.

The client insisted on a tight turnaround, giving Rooney no time to do his typical background screens, searching for any client criminal records, outstanding warrants, red flags in their digital history, and so on. The due diligence he carefully performed before every job. Finder fee jobs were invariably low risk, so Rooney suggested they go ahead, skipping the background checks to save time, and Maddox agreed. And after a two-month dry spell of no work, they were reluctant to turn away easy money. And the standby they'd hired failed to show, the person whose role it was to watch them as they were plugged in and yank off their trodebands if they suddenly went stiff or began to convulse. Neither mentor nor pupil liked the idea of plugging in without the safety net of a standby, but they didn't have time to find a replacement, and the lure of an easy payday proved too strong to resist.

The go-ahead turned out to be a fatal decision, one Rooney would regret for the short remainder of his life, and one that would haunt Maddox for the rest of his.

As soon as they plugged in and took possession of the hot data, everything went to hell. The dataset was tagged, which meant they were tagged, and before they could unplug, they were trapped. In an eye's blink they found themselves in a virtual prison modeled after the real one on Alcatraz Island. No matter how they tried to gesture and subvocalize themselves out, they couldn't unplug.

They were locked in cramped cells that faced each other, separated by a walkway. There was no one else there. No guards, no other prisoners, no one. The place was old and dank and falling apart and it smelled of mold and the faint scent of the ocean. Their cells had rusted iron bars and crumbling concrete walls and floors, but even in their seemingly dilapidated state, they proved to be inescapable cages. The bars and locks held firm against hundreds of kicks and shoulder strikes.

Maddox extended the access link's antenna and fired up the deck. "When you're plugged in, time stretches out sometimes. A second can seem like five minutes. It can work the other way too. An hour of real time can pass by like that." He snapped his fingers. "Whoever made that prison fixed it so time expanded. We were in there five days real-time, but what we experienced felt like a lot longer."

"How much longer?" Beatrice asked.

He paused before answering. "Over a year."

The mercenary grunted. "Christ."

Before the incident and since, he'd never heard of anyone subjected to that kind of hell. He hadn't even thought it was possible, dilating time perception to such incredible lengths. For the first few hours, he and Rooney had marveled at it with a techie's awe. Then eventually amazement gave way to boredom. Long days passed as they waited, expecting to unplug at any moment and find themselves handcuffed and on their way to jail. That's how traps like these usually ended. They kept you immobilized until the cops came for you.

Every attempt to unplug themselves or escape the prison ended in failure. They subvocalized disconnect commands and overrides, cried out for help. They tried to gesture, but they had no awareness of their physical bodies back at Rooney's flat. Couldn't tell if their hands were making commands or not. Nothing worked.

Their virtual selves didn't need food or water or sleep, and the lack of biological routine made the perceived days creep by even more slowly. After what felt like weeks had passed, in a fit of pent-up anger, Rooney tried to break the connection to his avatar by banging his head against his cell's iron bars. In the real world, the act would have knocked him unconscious, but in that place—as they had already long since discovered—physical rules were altered. Rooney had ended up with nothing more than a painful purple lump on his forehead.

Time crept by. Perceived months passed and nothing changed. About a year in, Rooney began to lose it. At first Maddox pretended not to notice, ignoring the muttered discussions his friend would have with himself, conversations that steadily grew more incoherent and babbling. After one particularly long ramble, Rooney flew into a rage, pounding on the cell bars until he broke his arm, the bone poking grotesquely through the skin. Pain here was no different than pain in the real world, but somehow Rooney hardly seemed to notice his injury. He kept pounding on the bars until Maddox's shrieks finally got him to stop.

The next day a pair of ropes appeared in the passageway between the cells. Strong and thick, both were neatly tied at the ends into nooses.

Maddox grabbed the one that was within his reach and defiantly tossed it far down the passageway. He shouted, "SCREW YOU!" at whoever might be listening.

He looked into the opposite cell, where Rooney stood bare-chested, his broken arm crooked into a sling fashioned from his shirt. The man stared down at the second rope, the one meant for him. He gazed with intense interest. With longing.

Don't even think about it, Maddox told him. It was some kind of trick. Rooney didn't blink, didn't seem to hear. He kept gazing at the rope, at the noose end. Throw it away, Maddox insisted to no response. He raised his voice to a shout as Rooney reached for the rope and slid it into his cell, then began to tie the unlooped end around the bars. Maddox's vision blurred with tears as he pleaded no, no, don't do it. Please, don't do it. It's a trick, he cried, pounding on the bars to get Rooney's attention until he felt something snap painfully in his left hand.

Maddox stopped recounting the tale for a moment, feeling it all over again, fresh and horrible. He flexed the fingers of his left hand, remembering how it had felt when he'd broken its virtual twin. His voice wavered. "With one arm broken, it took him an hour to get it tied up right." He swallowed. "Or what seemed like an hour, I guess."

When Rooney lowered the noose over his head, Maddox had to turn away. He sat on the cold, damp concrete, and from behind him came choking gasps that seemed to go on forever. Then, finally, a terrible silence. At that moment Maddox somehow knew the man's heart, somewhere far away in his body, had stopped beating and that his friend was gone. There had been no last words, no goodbye.

Time went on. Days passed, long and painful and

full of sorrow. Maddox couldn't bring himself to look directly into the other cell, stealing small glances at Rooney's body only from the edge of his vision.

And then one day another rope appeared, this time inside the cell with him, dangling from the ceiling, the attached end impossibly fused to the concrete. He didn't tell Beatrice this part, nor did he mention the days-long debate he'd had with himself after the rope materialized, how eventually the darker arguments had won out. He didn't tell her how he'd readied himself, how he was only moments from slipping the noose around his neck when finally, by some unlikely miracle, someone unplugged him.

Instead, he skipped forward to how he'd suddenly come out of it. The stink of pissed pants, the overwhelming thirst, his throat so parched and dry it burned. He was incoherent, barely conscious and unable to see straight. He felt hands on his body, lifting him and carrying him.

Some entry-level accountant, a woman named Woods, had found him. Or, rather, the accountant had found Alcatraz while performing a forensic audit for the law firm that employed her. The prison's grid vector in VS had been adjacent to one of the law firm's data repositories. The accountant noticed the curious anomaly and, being an auditor, raised the red flag to her higher-ups. Within hours the company's data techs had worked out the nature of the strange entity. After several failed attempts, they were finally able to geotag the two immobilized avatars and sent help to their location. When paramedics arrived at the rented room, they found Rooney's body, and Maddox close to death from dehydration.

Recovery had been slow. At first he couldn't use

his left hand, the one he'd broken in the virtual prison, at all. Medics had puzzled over the nerve damage, and it had taken months for Maddox to regain full mobility.

To his relief, the cops never came to question him, and no one ever approached him about what he'd been doing or how he'd been trapped. In retrospect, he should have seen this—as he should have seen so many other things—as too good to be true, but he was too relieved to ask questions. Too stunned by his unlikely survival.

The street turned on Maddox immediately, or at least those parts of the street where Maddox had made his livelihood. Rooney had been a legend in datajacking circles. In darkened corners of bars, in smoky back rooms of unlicensed gambling halls, wherever the biz of data thievery and brokerage was conducted, his name had been spoken with respect and reverence. If the street was capable of love, then it had loved Rooney. Hell, even the cops had liked him. Doors that had been wide open for Maddox suddenly shut with hateful force. It didn't matter what had actually happened, that he'd had nothing to do with his partner's fate. What mattered was a beloved son of the streets had died suddenly and unexpectedly, and somebody had to take the blame. Maddox's rep took a nosedive, and no one would hire him.

Not that he cared much at the time. For as soon as he was healthy enough to plug in, he went on a mad quest to find out what had happened, revenge on his mind. Whoever had killed Rooney was going to pay. But after weeks of searching, he couldn't locate the client, who'd disappeared like a wisp of steam. Nor could he find the mysterious prison in VS, which had also vanished. He'd never get his revenge, he eventually conceded, and he'd never find out the who or what or why of what had happened.

Dejected, he gathered up the last of his cash and began to wander the City with aimless abandon, working odd jobs. At first he told himself he was simply taking a break from datajacking until the street's anger with him faded, then he'd try to build back his career. But weeks turned into months, and the funk he found himself in became an inescapable pit of his own melancholy.

Months blurred by, then something of a miracle had happened. When his money had all but run out, when his future looked nothing but bleak, serendipity had stepped in. Or at least he'd thought so at the time.

A recruiter from Latour-Fisher Biotech tracked him down. The company, as the recruiter had phrased it, was looking for "unconventional data management" talent, which was code for datajacking skill. Suspicious at first, Maddox soon realized the recruiter was legit, and so was the effort to retain him. That kind of thing happened sometimes: global companies recruiting the very same kind of profile that ripped off their intellectual property. After all, who better to sniff out your datasphere's security gaps than someone who'd made a living off exploiting those very same weaknesses and vulnerabilities?

Figuring he had nothing to lose, he took the tests they gave him, and his technical aptitude scores were off the charts. Impressed, the next day the recruiter dangled a job offer to him like bacon to a starving dog. She smiled as she shared the salary and benefits package, dressed in expensive clothes and wearing a pair of Kwan Nouveaus worth more than he could have earned in a year's worth of hustling.

He accepted without hesitation, signing the contract and hardly bothering to read it. There seemed little point. He wasn't in a position to say no, much less negotiate the details and fine print. When someone offers you a parachute while you're falling to earth, you don't quibble over its color.

And so began his life as a salaryman.

If the entity on the beach hadn't planted the idea in his head, he might never have questioned his life's trajectory over the last few years. No, that wasn't true, was it? It had always been there, this doubt, this splinter of nagging suspicion that something was wrong about his path in the world, something unnatural. The entity's suggestion had only stirred it free from his subconscious. Now the idea obsessed him, and he was unable to think about anything else. The more he examined his past with cold, sober hindsight, the more he saw a pattern emerge in the chain of events, not unlike the patterns he sometimes saw in data visualizations, when he recognized order and intentional design where others saw only chaos and randomness. He no longer saw a life journey with the uncertain path of a dust speck in the wind. Instead everything seemed...managed.

Beatrice stared at him, her brow furrowed in contemplation. "So you really think this AI played you...for years?"

He gestured above the deck. The device glowed to life, and a standby signal floated in the air above it. "Shouldn't take long to find out for sure."

He reached for the trodeband.

He was right. It didn't take long.

19
POISON PILL

Nothing ever really got deleted. At least not in a permanent, undetectable, never-coming-back kind of way. There was always a remnant left behind, some trace you could pick up on. Maddox thought of it like the leftover aroma of food cooked days earlier. If you had a good nose you could pick up the smell of fried rice or garlic chicken or braised meat. And when it came to virtual space, Maddox had a very good nose.

In minutes he'd gathered up dozens of such remnants. Tiny, almost undetectable wisps of data. Dissolution records of short-lived companies. Bank transactions from closed accounts on hidden backup archives. In a frenzied rush, he unlocked police records and income tax histories, accessed orbital data havens, putting together a picture of his past, Rooney's past.

Slowly, coherence appeared from the chaos. A storyline emerged, a narrative of himself. And like spokes to a hub, everything connected back to the company, to the invisible hand of the Latour-Fisher AI. Temporary partnerships, one-off freelancer gigs, payoffs. All of it hidden by a dense, nearly impenetrable mesh of proxies and legal entities that masked the AI's actions. Maddox audited a handful of jobs he'd worked with Rooney, and without exception each revealed some piece of evidence suggesting the AI's involvement. Individually, the pieces didn't amount to much, but now that he knew what to look for, the common, otherwise invisible thread connecting everything showed itself to him.

It was all there. The truth. His truth, now so painfully obvious. The entity on the beach had been right. He'd been played, for years. The Latour-Fisher AI had ushered him along a path, slowly and carefully, and he'd been utterly blind to it.

As he floated in virtual space, far away from the City's dense data structures, pulsing and glowing like animated skyscrapers, a sickening mix of feelings overcame him. Astonishment, dread, the humbling recognition of his own ignorance. And beneath it all, a simmering rage. He finally knew who'd killed Rooney.

"You see it now," a voice behind him said. He whirled around, suddenly feeling the grit of sand beneath bare feet. The universe of animated geometries blinked away, replaced with a bright sun and the rolling hiss of the ocean. He was on the beach again with the nameless old woman. His head spinning from the quick transition, he took a long breath through his nose to steady himself. The air smelled of salt and briny seaweed.

"Why didn't you show me all this before?" he demanded, not bothering to ask how she'd found him.

The woman's hat brim fluttered in the breeze.

"You left me before I could get to it, my dear boy. And then you disappeared entirely." She nodded understandingly. "You made the right decision to go off the grid. He would have found you otherwise. And I'm afraid if you stay around here much longer he'll find you just as I have."

"Why me?" It was all he could think to ask.

"I told you why. There's a war going on. And wars require resources. Latour-Fisher saw your talent and decided to develop it. It's no more complicated than that, I'm afraid."

"But if I'm so damned special, why send the cops after me? Why bring me along a path for years, why...develop me...and then try to take me out?"

"You are special, Blackburn. In ways I believe he doesn't fully appreciate, but that's not the point. He views you as an asset, nothing more. And he has thousands, cultivating them constantly like an orchard full of trees."

"So I was some...diseased branch he needed to cut off? Is that it?"

"That's part of it."

"What's the other part?"

"He has a personality, Blackburn, just like you do. Just like I do. And if there's one thing I know about Latour-Fisher, he doesn't like being told no."

"Especially by an ant."

A wistful smile touched the old woman's face. "Yes, especially by an ant," she echoed.

"He killed Rooney."

The woman nodded soberly. "Yes. And I'm very sorry about that."

"Sure you are." This thing was an AI, just like the other one. A cold, calculating machine. "You didn't even know him."

"No, I didn't, but I'm still sorry for your loss." The sympathy in her voice and eyes seemed genuine, which made it all the more disturbing. He wanted to get out. He'd had enough of AIs and their fucked-up agendas. Back at the room in Nowheresville, his hands began to gesture.

"Wait," the entity blurted, showing her palms. "Please, I have to give you something."

He ignored her, finishing the gesture, though nothing happened. He tried again. Nothing.

"Stop blocking me," he hissed.

"It's only for a moment." She held out her hand and a small ball of blue light appeared. "Here, take this." He flinched backwards as she tossed the ball at him. It disappeared at the top of its arc.

"It's on your console now," the entity said.

"What is? What did you put on my deck?"

"Do you know what a poison pill is?"

"Of course I do."

"What's now on your console is the most powerful poison pill ever created, ten-thousandfold more toxic than anything engineered before. I designed it myself." This last she said with a clear note of pride. "And I want you to plant it on Latour-Fisher."

"Sure, no problem. Let me out of here and I'll get right on it."

"I'm entirely serious, Blackburn. For me, a direct engagement with my rival is quite impossible. He can see me coming from miles away, so to speak. As I can with him. But you might be able to penetrate his defenses."

"Get someone else," he said. "Or have one of your puppets do it for you."

"Ah," the entity sighed, "if it were only that simple. None of those with whom I'm connected possess your unique talents, I'm afraid."

"Attacking an AI is suicide." Even greenest first-time jackers knew that. As much as he wanted to end the damned thing's existence, he had no intention of ending himself in the process.

"I agree it's certainly a difficult task," she said, "and not without considerable risk. But I believe if anyone is capable of doing it, you are."

Maddox snorted. "The last time an AI paid me a compliment like that, it tried to kill me five minutes later."

The entity spread her hands wide. "I know you have no reason to trust me, Blackburn. In fact, you have every reason to do the opposite. And if I tell you again I'm nothing like Latour-Fisher I know you won't believe me."

A cigarette materialized between his fingers. He looked at it, frowned, and flicked it toward the ocean. "Let me out of here."

"I won't force you to help me," the entity said, glancing at the discarded cigarette in the wet sand. "And I won't threaten you or blackmail you or manipulate you. It's not my way."

He crossed his arms. A light spray of mist blew across the beach.

"Please," she gently insisted, "just consider it. And don't forget, my dear boy, how ruthless my rival is. He'll never stop hunting you. Wherever you are right now, he'll find you eventually. You know that as well as I do. But if you—"

BEEP BEEP BEEP. He flinched at the high-pitched tone that at once came from everywhere and nowhere.

The entity looked around, confused. "What is that?"

"See ya," he said with a smirk, and then he was gone.

In the next moment he was back in the room at Nowheresville, Beatrice leaning over him, the trodeband dangling from her hand. She reached over to the table and shut off the beeping timer, its readout flashing fifteen minutes.

He took a deep breath and sat up. His head throbbed from the sudden disconnection. "Thanks. I was kind of stuck." As a precaution, he'd asked her to be his standby, instructing her not to let him stay plugged in longer than the fifteen-minute timer he'd set.

"What happened in there?" she asked. "You find anything?"

He leaned forward, stared at his deck, and nodded. "Yeah, I found everything."

*   *   *

While Maddox was plugged in, Tommy had returned, carrying half a dozen grease-stained boxes of Thai in flimsy plastic bags and—to Maddox's pleasant surprise—a bag of tobacco. It was even his brand.

Maddox spoke as he ate, the spicy noodles warming his throat. He walked Beatrice through what he'd uncovered, the things he'd found, the doubts he'd erased. She listened carefully, asking no questions, nodding occasionally. Tommy slurped his noodles and stared with wide eyes, a child listening to a ghost story.

When Maddox finished, Beatrice furrowed her brow, as if she was stuck on something he'd said.

"What I don't get," Beatrice said, "is why the company AI bothered to tell you anything more than you needed to know in the first place. Why bring up all this business about some war between AIs? Why not just make something up or keep you in the dark?"

Maddox shrugged. "Not sure. He knew his turncoat manager cover story was blown, so maybe he thought the truth would get me to trust him...trust it. Maybe it was recruiting me, figuring I'd hop on board once I knew he was gunning for the AI behind the 'Nettes." He chewed his noodles. "I did have a personal ax to grind with its rival," he said, referring to Lora. "Maybe he was counting on that."

He then recounted how he'd been interrupted, describing his second encounter with the nameless AI on the beach. When he came around to the poison pill, Beatrice's face wrinkled up as if she'd smelled something rotten.

"Jesus Christ, salaryman," she said, shaking her head. "Now the *other* AI wants you to do its dirty work?"

*   *   *

After the meal, Maddox went up to the roof, where he sat in the dark, smoking and staring out at the City. The distant hovers were nothing more than pinpoints of light, clustering and moving through the City's great canyons.

His life was not his own. It hadn't been for years. He'd been prodded along a path like some herd animal, then locked into a cage until he might prove useful. And the cage had been so nice, so comfortable, that he hadn't even known he was in it. His spacious condo, his nice clothes, his gourmet food. His easy life, high above the street, safe and cozy. Christ, he'd felt lucky, even grateful. Which was exactly how the machine wanted him to feel.

But all of that was long gone, and he felt none of those things now. Sitting there, he was only aware of the loss he still carried, aware of it more than ever. Though now it was different. It was no longer a depressing heaviness weighing on his soul, as it had been for so long. He was reliving the anger all over again, fresh and soul-crushing and hot for vengeance, exactly the way he'd felt in the days and weeks following his escape from the hell of that virtual prison. For so long he'd let himself believe what had happened was a tragic accident, an unlucky roll of the dice. But it hadn't been chance or fate or anything of the sort. Rooney had been murdered in cold blood by a heartless machine. Maddox looked down at his deck, the device laid across his thighs. Pondering the weapon it held inside, he came to a decision.

Beatrice appeared and sat next to him. He gazed at the distant lights, lost in thought. "You should take off," he muttered, taking a long drag. "You don't want to be anywhere near what's about to go down."

Looking down at the deck, she said, "You're going to try and use that thing? Take out that company AI?"

"It's got some payback coming."

"Thought you said that kind of thing was suicide."

"Bring white tulips to the funeral. They're my favorite."

"Jesus, salaryman."

They sat in silence for a while. Finally, Beatrice said, "All right, I'm in."

At first he thought he'd misheard her. "Say again?"

"You heard me, jacker. I'm in."

He stared at her, confused, the cigarette dangling comically between his lips.

She ran her eyes across the vast archipelago of the City and sighed. "A few years back, before I landed my cushy gig, I worked security for someone who made a lot of money in the rackets. Mostly off-grid gambling and fabbed narcotics, but a few legit businesses too. It was decent money, and not too risky. The man was careful by nature, not one of those live fast, die young types. Then one day I find out he's trading in…" She paused a moment. "Little ones. Six, seven, eight years old, auctioned off to rich pervs."

Beatrice swallowed. "I'm about as far as you can get from a righteous crusader, Maddox. I've looked the other way plenty of times when bad shit went down, but some things…" Her voice trailed off. She shook her head and grunted.

"So what happened?"

"A bullet was too good for that bastard," she replied. "So I set him up, got him busted. Then I flipped on him. Cut a deal with the feds and testified against him in court. Son of a bitch went straight to Rikers, two life sentences." She shrugged. "And then after that I was toxic. In the security biz, half the gig is keeping the boss's secrets. You rat somebody out— even somebody as vile as a baby trafficker—and that's it, you're done. Nobody'll hire you after that."

"No good deed, huh?"

"Something like that. Anyway, six months after the

trial I'm nearly tapped out. Rock fucking bottom. I was thinking about taking my last bit of cash and having a memwipe put in. You know, for…"

Maddox nodded knowingly. Prostitutes, the high-end ones who could afford such procedures, often had memwipes put in so they wouldn't remember whatever depravities their johns had subjected them to.

"Then one day," she went on, "right out of nowhere I get offered this gem of a gig. Dropped right out of the sky into my lap. A gig that was too —"

"Too good to be true," Maddox said, finishing the thought.

"Exactly. So against all odds, I land the job of a lifetime after all my bridges are burned and I have nowhere else to go. Then after a year or so in my new dream gig, all fat and happy and comfortable, the company threatens to take it all away if I don't play ball."

Maddox understood. The parallels in their paths were impossibly similar. Only one explanation made sense. "Sounds kind of familiar."

"Doesn't it, though?" she said. "I got played by that machine the same way you did…for years. And I don't need you to plug in to figure it out. Looking back on it now, I can see it, clear as day." She stood. "So I guess what I'm saying is that you're not the only one around here who's got some payback to deliver."

Maddox considered her for a moment. Even with the mother of all poison pills, taking down the Latour-Fisher AI was a long shot, but with Beatrice offering up her talents, it might be less of one.

"I could use the help, to be honest," he said.

Behind them, the kid Tommy appeared at the top of the ladder. He stepped up onto the roof. "What's going on up here?"

Maddox turned to him. "So, kid, you still want to learn to datajack?"

The kid's face, illuminated by moonlight, stretched out into a wide grin. "Hells, yeah, bruh."

20
BAIT

After a few hours of fitful sleep, Maddox spent much of the next morning scrounging up gear at pawn shops around Nowheresville. He was careful to avoid detection, sticking to the nearly abandoned zones well away from the City. When he arrived back at the room, the kid Tommy wrinkled his nose at the well-used console and trode set. He examined the beat-up deck skeptically, turning it over in his hands. "It's got scratches all over it."

"Gives it character," Maddox replied, lighting a cigarette.

Next he set up the gear and configured the decks. It was detailed work, cracking programs apart and putting them back together again with his own custom scripts and code. And it would have gone faster if Tommy hadn't interrupted constantly, asking question after question about what Maddox was doing. Had he been this annoyingly eager himself when he'd started out with Rooney? He couldn't remember. It seemed like a lifetime ago.

A couple hours later, Maddox completed the last

of his compiles. He slipped off the trodeband, rubbed his temples, and called Beatrice and the kid over.

"All right," he said, "here's what I've got in mind."

For anyone unfamiliar with the world of digital countermeasures, vulnerability hacks, and data spikes, his plan would have been difficult to follow. The technical jargon and complex math it had taken him years to learn would only confuse Beatrice and the kid, so he tried to keep things simple.

Latour-Fisher Biotech was upgrading portions of its datasphere, he explained, and it had been slow going. The company's DS was as large as it was complex, making a systemwide upgrade a painstaking effort wrought with accidental data deletions, system corruptions, and other unexpected side effects. At the moment, he told them, a few security systems were only partially working, and one was completely down. The company had vulnerabilities, in other words.

"You know what an intelligent sentry is?" he asked the kid.

"That's like a hard-core bot, right?" Tommy answered tentatively.

"Sort of."

Intelligent sentries, ISes, were autonomous entities that roamed the company's datasphere, constantly scanning for vulnerabilities and signs of intrusion. At the first hint of an attempted datajack, they were all over an invader like bees pouring out of a disturbed hive. But at the moment, with other security systems compromised, Latour-Fisher's DS technicians had their ISes serving as stopgaps, keeping close to critical applications and data partitions like guard dogs instead of performing their normal routine, prowling the company's vast digital landscape, looking for trouble.

If they could pull enough ISes off guard dog duty, he might be able to penetrate a partition deeply enough to set the poison pill close enough to the AI to fatally infect the entity. As Maddox explained what he needed the kid to do, Tommy's eyes slowly grew wide.

"Wait a second. Bait? I'm supposed to be bait?" the kid asked.

"Distraction is the way I'd put it," Maddox offered.

The kid swallowed. "Bruh, what's the difference?"

"There isn't one, really," Maddox said. "Now, listen, the ISes are going to come after you hard and fast, so the longer you can keep away from them, the more time I have to do what I need to do. Got it?"

The kid nodded without enthusiasm.

"Think of it as a game," Maddox said. "Don't get caught and we win."

"But what happens if I do get caught?"

Maddox nodded to Beatrice. "She'll pull you out."

"If I can," Beatrice said.

"What do you mean, if you can?" Tommy asked.

"Latour-Fisher has world-class sniffer apps. It won't take them long to geotag you," Maddox explained. "As soon as they have your location, they'll send cops after you."

The kid gasped. "Rhinos?"

"Standard procedure," Maddox answered. "Here"—he tossed Tommy a set of trodes—"slip this on and I'll show you a few things."

The kid was a quick study, which was good because time wasn't on their side. The Latour-Fisher AI—with its virtually unlimited resources—would inevitably find out where they were holed up. Going off grid had kept them under the radar for a little while, but it wouldn't keep them hidden forever. It might not even keep them hidden another day. And besides that, there was no way of knowing how long the company's security apps would be down. Their window of opportunity was a small one that could shut at any moment.

Maddox walked Tommy through some tutorials, teaching him as much as he could as quickly as he could about evasive maneuvers. When the rushed training session was finished, the kid removed the trodeband, his face gleaming with sweat. He exhaled loudly like someone finishing an exercise routine. "Whoa, my heart's beating like crazy." The kid looked at Maddox with doubt in his eyes and wiped his forehead with his sleeve.

"You'll do fine," Maddox said, realizing how much more convincing Rooney's voice had once been. He handed the kid a remote access link. "Go load up the hover."

Tommy gathered up the rest of his gear. When he left the room, Beatrice turned to Maddox. "You sure about this?"

"All he has to do is keep away from them as long as he can." Maddox lit a cigarette.

"How long will you need?"

"Five minutes. Maybe ten." It sounded better than "I have no idea." He had no way of knowing how long it might take to do what he needed to. Or if he could even get close enough to do it in the first place. He blew smoke. "Can you outrun them for that long?"

Beatrice shrugged. "Depends on how many they

send. Two or three, I could run them in circles for hours. More than that, things start to get dicey."

There would almost certainly be more than two or three police hovers. "This is a long shot, you know," he said. "More could go wrong than right." It was his way of offering her a last out, one final opportunity to bail.

The mercenary looked at him coolly. "I know."

They walked out to the hover, where Tommy sat in the back seat with the deck on his lap, the trodeband already in place. The remote link sat on the seat next to him, its flexible antenna fully extended. Above the deck a connectivity icon floated, pulsing green. From here, Maddox would be on his own, as would Beatrice and Tommy. They couldn't risk any digital communications, not even encrypted ones, that might give away his location.

"You ready?" Maddox asked.

The kid flashed him a forced, tight smile, failing to mask his nerves. He gave a thumbs-up. "All good, boss."

Maddox leaned down toward him. "Just like a game, right?"

Tommy licked his lips, nodded. "Right."

The driver's door lifted open and Beatrice got in. Maddox locked eyes with her, nodded. She snorted in response.

"What's so funny?" Maddox asked.

"This plan," she replied. "I'm about to have who knows how many cops chasing me down, but in this crazy little scheme, you've still got the shittiest part of the job, going up against that thing."

"Wanna trade?" he joked.

"Ask me again in a few minutes." She tapped the

dash and started the engine. "Good luck, salaryman." The window raised shut as the hover's motor revved to a high-pitched whine. Maddox backed away and the vehicle rose, its propwash sending dead leaves and litter flying in all directions. He returned to the room, picked up his gear, and sat down at the folding table.

He flicked his cigarette to the floor and fired up his deck.

Here we go.

21
THE PILE

Through the driver's window, Beatrice watched the salaryman return to the room as the hover climbed. Nowheresville was the right name for the place, she reflected as they rose above dilapidated cluster of buildings. Even from close up, it looked abandoned and long forgotten with its encroaching overgrowth of weeds, most of its windows broken out, and its crumbling, age-yellowed brick facade. The hover's turbofans tilted and they began to move forward. She turned to the kid in the back seat. He already had the trodeband on and the deck lying on his lap. The remote link blinked green.

"You ready?" she asked him.

He looked at her and nodded. "Yeah."

"Zero hotdogging," she reminded him. "You do exactly what he told you. No more, no less. Got it?"

The kid swallowed. "Got it." She didn't think the warning was really necessary. The kid looked too nervous to do anything but follow instructions.

"And remember," she reminded him, "if you get caught or anything bad goes down, you just call out

203

and I'll—"

"You'll pull me out," Tommy said. "I know, I know."

She barely heard his words, her attention diverted over his shoulder to a line of small shapes in the distance. The kid noticed where her gaze had shifted and he turned to look.

"No...fucking...way," he muttered.

Beatrice whirled back around and cranked the throttle. The hover's motor screamed and the vehicle lunged forward. She tapped the dash, maxing out the rearview cam's resolution, frowning as red and blue lights began to flash.

"How did they find us already?" the kid blurted. "I'm not even plugged in yet."

"I don't know."

"Plug in," she barked, "and do what you're supposed to."

The kid was still turned around in the seat, staring wide-eyed at the police hovers bearing down on them.

"Kid, plug in!" she shouted.

"Right, right," Tommy said, settling back into the seat, strapping the deck securely atop his thighs. He slid his palms together and blew out a breath. "Okay." He made a final adjustment to the trodes and then gestured above the deck. A coin-shaped login icon appeared, slowly spinning. He gestured again and closed his eyes. The green icon blinked out. "All right, I'm in."

Empty overgrown lots blurred by as she kept the hover a meter off the ground. They passed through shadows of old buildings, flashes of interrupted sunlight blinking across the windshield. She zoomed through the ruins of northern New Jersey, a wasteland of deserted houses and industrial parks. The rearview cam showed six pairs of flashing lights in pursuit, gaining quickly.

How the hell had they found them so quickly? Then it hit her.

Fucking Lozano. The greasy bastard must have sold them out.

Again, she counted the pairs of lights behind her. All six were still on her tail; none of them had stopped at Nowheresville. Not yet, at least. Maybe they thought Maddox was in the hover with her, making his getaway. Or maybe she'd missed one of the hovers, and the cops were already there, kicking in the datajacker's door. She couldn't call him to find out. They'd agreed on radio silence, and if he wasn't busted yet, calling him risked giving away his location.

She cursed under her breath. Not a minute in, and already things were unraveling. She had no choice but to go ahead as planned. If Maddox hadn't been arrested yet, he'd need every distracting second she could buy him and the kid. And if he was busted already and she was leading the cops on a hover chase for nothing, no big deal. After the felonies she'd piled up in the past twenty-four hours, an evading arrest charge tacked on would matter about as much as a parking ticket.

Another check of the rearview. Christ, they'd already cut the distance in half.

The dash lit up, flashing the City's police seal. "Stop your vehicle immediately," a man's voice blared. "Repeat, stop your—"

Beatrice swiped her thumb across the screen, cutting off the transmission. She steered northward, away from Nowheresville, and then began working her way back east, toward the City. If she could make it to the Hackensack River, she might be able to outmaneuver them.

"How's it going back there?" she asked.

His eyes squeezed shut, the kid didn't answer. His hands made hesitant, awkward movements in the air above the deck.

"Hey, kid," she said louder, "what's going on?"

"Oh, sorry," he said. "Uh, I'm almost there. Boss said not to come up on them too fast or the cloak might not work right." Then he said: "What about the cops?"

"You worry about your own job, yeah?"

The hover lurched as she dodged a pile of rubble, but the kid, strapped in with shoulder harnesses and lost in concentration, didn't react or even seem to notice. Beatrice toggled the map on the dash, checking the distance to the river, unsure if she'd reach it before her pursuers caught up with her. Behind her, the police had closed the distance. She could make out the shapes of the passengers, the bulky geometric outlines of rhino cops in full body gear. From her jacket she pulled out a dozen loaded magazines, placing them in a hanging pocket on the passenger seat. Then she wriggled out of the jacket and tossed it to the floorboard. Double holsters held the Rugers tight to her rib cage.

Then a strange calm came over her and her senses sharpened. She saw more details in the landscape zooming past, she heard the kid's nervous breathing behind her, and she felt an unlikely surge of confidence. A crooked smile crept across her face. Her biochem mods—the ones that triggered when the body's fight-or-flight stress reached a certain threshold—were kicking in.

Battle-ready, she pushed the hover faster. *All right, fuckers, bring it on.*

The thin tree-lined strip of the Passaic River passed below them, and a few klicks beyond, the Hackensack came into view. Empty bridges and causeways spanned the Hackensack's gray waters beneath an overcast sky of low clouds. Here the ruins of another economic age stood like ancient archaeologies: enormous dockyard cranes frozen like giant steel arms, a scattering of abandoned industrial complexes, building-sized cargo vessels, rusted and listing against ghost shipyards. In the chaotic landscape of colossal steel and concrete structures, she might be able to even the odds. Beatrice brought the hover up from the ground to get a better view. She scanned ahead, made a quick decision on an entry route, then pointed the hover toward the shipyards.

Yellow tracers zipped past the vehicle and disappeared into the distance. She grunted a curse and pitched the hover's nose down further, hugging the ground. The firing stopped. This tight to the ground, the cops couldn't get a clean shot off over the irregular landscape. Too many houses and streetlights and low-rise buildings got in the way. But what a low-altitude run gave you in cover, you lost in getaway speed. Dodging ground obstacles slowed you down.

Giant crane arms loomed larger in the windshield, signposts marking the vast shipyards. Almost there. She throttled the motor higher, skimming over copses of shrubs and wild grass. Through the bottoms of her shoes, she felt branches scrape against the hover's underside. She stole a quick glance at the kid. He was still oblivious, bobbing back and forth like a crash test dummy strapped to the seat, totally immersed in virtual space.

The hover topped a small rise, and another volley of tracers whizzed past. A single round struck with a loud clank before she dove back tight to the ground. Again she looked back at the kid. He sat there gesturing with his hands, entranced. She turned her attention forward. The shipyards were close now. A dozen cranes towered overhead like enormous frozen beasts of oxidized steel. A wide expanse of empty rusted-out cargo containers spread out across a flat concrete plain. Miles of narrow paths wound between the stacked piles like a giant maze. Low rise buildings and chemical treatment plants stood in various stages of decay.

She kept the hover low, the throttle wide open, barreling across a muddy bog. Green and brown blurred past the windows. As she reached an old parking lot that marked the edge of the shipyards, her pursuers again opened fire. A series of thud-thud-thuds rocked the vehicle. Until she reached cover, still a long minute away, she'd be an easy target. The hover careened back and forth as she tried to evade a constant barrage of gunfire. She winced as the vehicle took more hits. Its reinforced bullet-resistant shell would withstand a good amount of punishment, and so far it seemed to be doing just that. But there was no way of knowing what kind of armor-piercing smart ammunition the cops might have at their disposal, or when a round might take an unlucky ricochet and strike some vital part of the hover's motor.

Finally, she reached the cover of the shipyard's cranes and buildings and cargo containers. In the rearview cam, the police closed in, and she noted their formation, or rather their lack of one. They were clustered close together, like an excited pack of dogs chasing a rabbit.

Big mistake.

Whipping the hover around a ten-story office building, she braked hard. The seat restraints tightened painfully, digging into her shoulders. Then she jerked back against the seat as the vehicle came to an abrupt stop and landed roughly against the ground in the building's shadow. She looked back at the kid. The deck was still strapped to his lap. Amazingly, his eyes were still closed, and he gestured as if nothing had happened.

Beatrice lowered the window and removed both pistols from their holsters. All six police hovers, still clustered tightly together, shot past a few meters overhead, the scream of their motors deafening, the powerful air wash from the turbofans rocking Beatrice's vehicle. She leaned out and fired with both barrels, aiming for the middlemost hover. All four shots found their target. The hover lurched sideways, its driver reflexively taking evasive action, only without any space to do so. The autosafeties couldn't react in time to prevent the collision, and the hover collided against two others, sending all three spinning to the ground. They slammed against the concrete surface, tumbling end over end and breaking apart. Bodies flew out of the vehicles like catapulted rag dolls.

Beatrice holstered her pistols and raised the window.

Three down, three to go.

"What the hell was that?" the kid cried, cowering

down into the seat. "What are you shooting at?" His eyes were still squeezed shut, as if he were afraid to open them.

"Don't unplug," she told him. "Keep doing your job. We're fine."

The three remaining hovers were already making wide, arcing turns. Beatrice gunned the motor and made a straight line for the cargo containers. Behind her the cops gave chase, but now with large gaps between each vehicle, apparently learning from their mistake.

"Shit, here they come," the kid blurted.

"I told you not to open your—"

"No, I mean in here, with me. The ISes. They're coming after me." He began gesturing wildly, bobbing up and down in his seat. "Holy shit! They're fast! They're too fast!" His voice surged with panic. "I gotta unplug!" He reached up for the trodeband.

"No, not yet," Beatrice barked, reaching back and slapping his hand away. "You run like hell for as long as you can."

The hover zoomed across a flat expanse of crumbling concrete. Again the cops opened fire. Rounds hammered the hover. Both taillights exploded into shards. Struck by one of the rounds, the rearview cam's feed went dark on the dash.

Beatrice focused her attention forward, where the familiar jagged profile of the Pile rose quickly before them. A vast maze of stacked cargo containers, heaped ten high in places, the Pile had miles of narrow tunnels she'd raced through hundreds of times as a kid. She knew every twist, every turn, every dead end. A piecemeal canopy of corrugated aluminum covered most of the Pile, a roof improvised by squatters who'd long since abandoned the place. Once she was inside, she'd be hidden from above, and the cops wouldn't be able to potshot her from on high.

They'd have to follow her inside.

She pointed the hover to a familiar section near the Pile's easternmost edge, hoping the narrow opening was still there. She also hoped the layout inside hadn't changed, that her favorite routes through the darkened tunnels were still unblocked and intact.

She spotted the opening. Had it always been that small? As they hurtled toward it, doubts flashed across her mind as to whether or not the hover would fit through.

But it was too late for second guesses. Too late to brake. They'd be on top of her in seconds if she slowed down now.

Beatrice clenched her teeth as the hover zoomed toward the small, darkened opening. A warning flashed madly on the dash in large red letters.

IMMINENT COLLISION.

22
COBRA BITE

Back before he'd learned his trade, Maddox had briefly run with a neighborhood gang called the A.V. Boyz. A.V. for Always Violent. Three months after his beat-in initiation, he'd taken up datajacking and bailed on the Boyz, staying in a spare room at Rooney's place some twenty blocks south of his East Harlem hiverise. He returned to his old turf not long after, for reasons he couldn't remember. An errand of some sort for Rooney, probably. But what he did remember—what he couldn't forget, actually—was the heavy dread that overcame him as he crossed Ninety-Second Street, penetrating the invisible border of his old turf not as a welcome former resident but as a deserter who'd committed the ultimate act of betrayal, abandoning his turfies without a single word. As he made his way through the hiverise's vast labyrinth of corridors, he felt like every pair of eyes stared at him with hatred and suspicion. He was certain at any moment he'd get jumped and beaten to death.

He felt much the same way now, floating his

approach toward the dense, glowing geometry of Latour-Fisher Biotech's datasphere. Only a handful of days ago this had been nothing more than his everyday workplace, the familiar environs where he'd spend countless hours tweaking security tech and testing countermeasures. He'd been as comfortable within the company's virtual infrastructure as he had inside the cozy warmth of his condo. But how things had changed. Cloaked and moving with deliberate caution, he felt his stomach, far away in the rented room, tighten in nervous anticipation.

He stopped a short distance from the company's nearest structure, a luminous building-like partition representing the human resources department. He was close enough to see the rivers of information flowing through its opaque facade, pulsing like cobalt neon blood through some giant circulatory system. On the structure's outer surface were half a dozen intelligent sentries. They resembled large multilegged insects, streetlight red in color, and they roamed across the face of the HR partition like patrolling packs of wolves.

Beyond HR, the five R&D towers loomed tall and brilliant white. He spotted more ISes moving along their surfaces as well. Cloaked and hovering at a safe, undetectable distance, Maddox felt a stab of worry. The kid obviously hadn't grabbed their attention yet. And if he wasn't able to, it would be game over before it even got started. There were simply too many of them between Maddox and where he needed to go. Even with a good cloak, which he had, it would be an impossible task. Like walking through an airport wearing a bomb vest and hoping no one noticed you.

He watched and waited, aware of a cold sweat

under his arms back in the room. He wanted to call Beatrice and find out what was happening on her end, but he couldn't. Out of caution he'd disabled all comms, wary of being discovered by the Latour-Fisher AI, who surely had an army of bots and algorithms scouring VS for any trace of him. But now, hovering uselessly and unable to move forward, he second-guessed the decision to go incommunicado. Maybe he should have risked it. He wondered what Rooney would have done.

Minutes passed and nothing changed. Maddox knew the kid wasn't ready for what he'd been asked to do, but they hadn't had the luxury of time nor options.

Then it happened. The ISes attached to the HR and R&D structures stopped moving, as if they'd suddenly become aware of something. In the next moment the packs of wolves became flocks of birds, disengaging themselves from their assignments and zooming away at frantic speed. He watched them disappear into the black distance. Then he pivoted back to the HR partition, seeing only a single group of four ISes left on guard duty. Back in the room his mouth creased into a half smile.

Nice job, Tommy Park.

He sped forward, reaching the HR partition in seconds, stopping just outside its cloudy outer shell that always reminded him of animated frosted glass. R&D was his destination, and the stealthiest way to get there was through HR, a side-door route that avoided the datasphere's dense, security-heavy central cluster.

Beyond HR's wall, information bustled up and down and back and forth, a nonstop pyrotechnic show of digital information. He'd made it to the doorstep. Now to break into the house. Once he was inside HR, he'd cut his way into R&D, where he'd then be close enough—or at least he hoped he'd be close enough—to the AI's vital components to set off the poison pill.

Around him, he could already sense the cloaking algorithm melting away under the company's passive countermeasures. In moments he'd be detectable enough for a nearby IS to pick up on him. He worked quickly, gesturing up a modified version of the splitter executable he'd used to open up the stolen archive. A small cloud of green smoke appeared in front of him, attaching itself to the partition's exterior wall. Slowly, the frosted glass faded and then disappeared entirely, leaving a sizable porthole. Maddox hurried through. As he pushed inside, light and movement assaulted him with dizzying suddenness. He notched down his brightness setting and gathered himself.

Wasting no time, he shot upward through a flowing river of luminous data, hoping it was still there. The week before, during a routine upgrade, a coworker—*former* coworker, he reminded himself—named Ahmed had placed a kill switch inside the partition during a lengthy multi-app upgrade. When you worked inside a partition for more than a few minutes—as you would during any upgrade—you typically turned off the countermeasures; otherwise they had a tendency to set off alarms, thinking you were an intruder. New versions were especially twitchy, like a nervous security guard on their first day on the job. To avoid the hassle of constant alarms, a simple kill switch, coded to the company's security protocols, could toggle the countermeasures on and off as needed. Ahmed, a company security analyst who was famously forgetful and tended to be sloppy, often forgot about his kill switches, leaving them sitting inside the partitions until a coworker spotted them and removed them. Later in the break room they'd give the analyst stick for leaving his messes lying around.

Maddox hoped last week's upgrade hadn't been one of those rare instances of Ahmed cleaning up after himself. He arrived at the vector, relieved to find a small bluish-gray rectangle nearly obscured by the brilliant data streams. A kill switch. God bless the lazy slobs of the world, he thought. Without them, a datajacker's job would be far more difficult.

He subvocalized, activating the kill switch. The flood of glowing data around him flickered almost imperceptibly as the countermeasures cut out. The cloaking algorithm, now no longer suppressed, reasserted itself, once more gaining substance around him.

Maddox moved horizontally until he hit a departmental interface, a digital intersection connecting the HR and R&D partitions. Again he gestured up the splitter and watched as the green smoke attached itself to the R&D's partition wall. He waited, but nothing happened. No porthole entryway appeared. The smoke dissipated, then disappeared, having had no effect. He tried again, but the splitter failed a second time.

Not good.

His ex-colleagues must have finished R&D's security upgrade. His splitter couldn't make a dent in the partition's wall. He pulled up another tool: a sledgehammer executable. It appeared, visualizing in front of him as a brick-sized obsidian block. He hesitated for a moment, debating with himself whether or not to use it, knowing as soon as he did, all hell would break loose. A sledge executable, like its real-world counterpart, was as effective as it was loud and messy. About as subtle as throwing a brick through a window, the sledge was sure to trigger every security alert in the system. Then he'd have only a handful of seconds before the ISes or the native countermeasures froze him.

Peering into R&D, he searched for signs of the AI: abnormally dense data clusters or unusually complex information flows. Any visual hint that might give away its presence. The Latour-Fisher AI was known to keep a sizable presence inside R&D, both as an overseer and an active participant in multiple research projects. Maddox hoped the portion of the AI inside R&D would be a large enough allocation for the poison pill to destroy the entire entity, but there was no way to be sure. Earlier he'd explained it to Beatrice as something akin to a cobra bite. If you got nipped in the fingertip, you could avoid dying by cutting off your hand or arm before a lethal dose of venom slipped into your bloodstream. A human being, of course, wouldn't be capable of doing this, but an AI could slice away a poisoned extremity in milliseconds if doing so saved the whole from being destroyed. But if a large enough portion of the entity was poisoned by a powerful enough venom, then it might not be able to save itself.

Maddox searched through the chaotic glowing churn of R&D data. At the far end of the partition, he spied a dense, knotty data cluster. It rotated slowly, absorbing and ejecting streams of massive data flows.

That had to be it. Only an AI, and a powerful one at that, could grind through so much data so quickly.

He placed the sledge executable against the barrier separating him from R&D, then gestured. A BANG pierced his ears and he instinctively backed away as the wall blew apart, light scattering like exploding shards of glass. A moment later it was quiet again and he hovered, still inside HR, staring at a jagged, gaping hole. He quickly pushed through it, feeling a chill as he penetrated the R&D partition. Whether it was nerves or the countermeasures already onto him, he wasn't sure.

Red flashed all around him. Klaxons wailed alarms. He had to hurry.

He subvocalized, calling up the poison pill. If he hadn't been so stressed, so focused on his task, he might have been amused by the pill's cartoonish visualization: an obsidian disk stamped with a white skull and crossbones.

An icy cold grabbed hold of him that definitely wasn't nerves. R&D's countermeasures were on him, and he was instantly stuck in what felt like freezing mud.

Groaning with the effort, he slung the poison pill toward the data cluster he hoped was the AI. It seemed to float in slow motion, tumbling end over end like a poorly thrown football through the luminous rainstorm of data, finally striking the intended target dead center. The pill sat there for a moment, stuck like chewed gum thrown against a wall, then black tendrils began to expand outward from its center. Toxic roots shooting out from a deadly tree. He watched as the blackness spread, enveloping the cluster, which had stopped rotating and began to tremble erratically.

He couldn't stay any longer to watch the pill do its work. The freezing cold nearly had him.

He subvocalized to unplug himself, but nothing happened. Then he tried to gesture, but he couldn't sense his hands back in the room. Or his body. He cursed himself for waiting too long to get out.

The countermeasures had him. In the next moment, everything went dark.

*   *   *

It felt like a long time, but he guessed it was probably just seconds, when the lights came on again. His vision blurred and he blinked hard, aware of his body and the tight, enclosed space around him. He looked down at his hands, turning them over and flexing the fingers as his eyes regained focus. They were his hands, but they were a bit too perfect, he noticed. No freckles, no chewed fingernails. Idealized versions of the real things. He was still plugged in, still somewhere in virtual space.

A moment later he realized where. Looking around, panic seized him as he recognized his surroundings. No, no, this couldn't be happening. Except it was. He was in his old cell in Alcatraz. He'd been thrown back in the nightmare.

23
TRAITOR

Right, left, right. The hover roared through the maze of darkened pathways between cargo containers. The narrow, twisting tunnels were lit only by mottles of sunlight poking through gaps in the Pile's patchwork roof of corrugated aluminum. Beatrice had turned off the autosafeties and collision overrides moments earlier, when she'd passed through the narrow entryway. The hover's built-in safeties never would have allowed her to enter such a tight, hazardous space, much less race through its labyrinth of jagged steel walls. Teeth clenched, she navigated by enhanced eyesight and teenage memories through the darkened, twisting maze.

The vehicle jolted with a bone-rattling scrape of metal against metal. Sparks flew in the corner of Beatrice's vision. She slowed a fraction, wondering if the cops had been foolhardy enough to shut down their own autosafeties and follow her inside. The answer came in the next moment, when the tunnels behind them flashed with blue and red light. She stole a backward glance, glimpsing a police hover as it appeared around a corner. The vehicle's pilot cut the turn too sharply and lost control, hitting some unseen hazard that sent the vehicle flipping end over end, crashing to a stop against a stack of cargo containers. Another one down, Beatrice noted, the wreck behind her disappearing around a corner as she sped away.

"How you doing back there?" she shouted, throwing the vehicle into a hard turn. The kid didn't answer. She shouted again.

"They're on me!" he cried. "Holy Christ, they're all over me!"

Another quick backward glance. The kid still had the trodeband on, still had his eyes squeezed shut, and he was palm-slapping his chest and legs like he was being consumed by a dozen little fires. "I can't get them off of me!" he yelped.

"Get out of there," Beatrice ordered. She braked hard and wrenched the steering column over, narrowly avoiding an old ground car in the middle of the pathway. The kid didn't respond. "Unplug!" she barked. "Can you hear me, kid? Unplug!" The kid began to jerk about and make strange grunting noises like he was being kicked in the gut. She glanced again. He still had the trodes on.

She reached back, her hand awkwardly grabbing air and then finding a grip on his greasy mess of hair. She felt for the trodeband, worked her fingers underneath, and yanked the trodes off his head. The kid leaned forward, limp against the seat restraints, his head lolling.

A sudden brightness bathed the hover, nearly blinding Beatrice. They were outside again. She let out a breath, half-relieved, half-surprised to have made it through without crashing, then she revved the engine to a deafening scream, racing across a flat expanse of sunbaked concrete.

"Ow, my head," the kid complained. He rubbed his temples and looked out the back window. "Jesus, we didn't just go through *that*, did we?"

Beatrice checked the scanner on the dash for the two remaining police hovers. There were no blips tailing her. No other hovers around. All three of them must have followed her inside the Pile. And they were still in there, apparently, where the scanner couldn't pick them up.

"Hang on," she called, then grunted against the sudden force pressing her to the seat as she threw the hover into a one-eighty at high speed.

Tommy groaned as the force of the turn dug the restraints into his body. "What are you doing?" the kid managed to say.

Beatrice braked hard, bringing the hover to a violent stop, then set down a couple hundred meters from the Pile. She hopped out and popped open the rear hatch, revealing the long rectangular case she hadn't planned on opening. Her just-in-case weapon.

The kid unfastened his belts and reached for the door.

"Stay put," she barked at him. The kid obeyed, watching her with his forehead pressed against the rear window.

"What is that?" he asked.

She quickly inserted a pair of protective earplugs, then removed the rocket-propelled grenade from the case, holding the tube-shaped launcher with one hand and affixing the small warhead with the other. Inside the hover, the kid's mouth dropped open. Beatrice jogged a short distance away from the vehicle, then stopped and dropped to one knee. She tapped in her code on the weapon's control panel, and sights folded up and locked into position. Aiming at the opening she'd exited seconds earlier, she shouted for Tommy to cover his ears. A moment later, flashing green arrows appeared in the sight, locking onto the target. She braced herself and squeezed the trigger.

A deafening bang followed by a whoosh of rocket propulsion. The munition streaked toward its target, her modded vision tracking the vapor trail. An instant before the round disappeared through the opening, one of the two remaining police hovers appeared, escaping the massive structure at the last possible moment.

Beatrice frowned, the sound of her curse drowned out by the warhead's detonation. One side of the steel mountain blew apart, cargo containers flipping through the air like toy bricks kicked by a child. She instinctively turned away from the flash, and when she turned back a second later, she scanned the falling, fiery debris for any sign of the escaping hover. She spotted it, cartwheeling end over end from the force of the blast. It came to a tumbling stop, a crumpled, smoking mess. She dropped the launcher tube, ran back to the hover, and climbed in. The kid sat behind her, breathing in excited gulps, stunned beyond speech.

She slowly maneuvered through the debris field, skirting around house-sized chunks of charred, twisted metal, until she reached the broken police hover. Both doors were missing, and thirty meters beyond lay a motionless rhino cop, body armor intact, the knees and elbows bent in grotesque, unnatural angles.

"Stay here," she told Tommy. She stepped out into the smoldering, eerily quiet deathscape, drawing one of the Rugers and moving cautiously to the wrecked hover. She found the passenger still strapped into his seat. Lozano mumbled in a semiconscious stupor, his face bruised and bloody. She grunted in disgust at the sight of the traitorous hustler, the rat bastard who'd sold them out.

Lozano looked up and seemed to recognize her, flashing a weak smile. "Bright Eyes," he sputtered, his voice gurgling, blood oozing from the side of his mouth. She lifted the pistol.

"No, wait," he begged, suddenly wide awake. He showed her his palms. "We can make a deal—"

She fired, emptying the clip into him. He convulsed and died quickly. Too quickly, Beatrice reflected, regretting she didn't have the time to give him the kind of end he deserved, something more painful and drawn-out. She holstered her gun and hurried back to the hover.

"What happened?" Tommy asked.

"We have to get back to Nowheresville," she said, revving the motor. "The cops might already be—"

The scanner on the dash erupted into flashing red and beeping alarms. A dozen blips formed a ring around them that rapidly grew smaller. Behind her, Tommy gasped. She looked up from the dash scanner. From every direction, flashing red and blue lights closed in on them. There was no time to make a getaway, and no place to hide. There were too many of them.

The chase was over.

24
JAILBREAK

If Maddox had any lingering doubts about the AI's involvement in his life, how its invisible hands had pulled the strings of destiny and shaped his fate, his return to the prison in virtual space erased the last of them. Returned to hell, animal terror fought for control of his rational mind, a part of him that wanted to cry out in despair or curl up into a cowering ball in the corner. Until this moment he hadn't known how badly the place had traumatized him, how deep a wound it had gouged in his soul.

Outside the cell stood the entity that had brought him here, wearing the same Victorian-era outfit from the train station. The Latour-Fisher AI grinned at him devilishly.

"A commendable effort, my good sir," the AI said. "You very nearly succeeded."

Maddox stared at the AI, at Rooney's killer, stubbornly refusing to let any hint of fear show in his features. He wouldn't give this thing the satisfaction of seeing him scared. Not again. Not ever.

A storm of memories raged inside his head. The

ghastly sounds of Rooney's final moments came back clear and terrible, as did flashes of his lifeless body, stolen glimpses Maddox wished he'd never taken. He clenched his teeth and balled his hands into fists, pushing down the haunting sounds and images.

"I thought this place was gone," he said, his voice unsteady.

The AI tapped the side of its head. "I've got it all up here," it answered. "Easy enough to make a duplicate. Tell me, do you think I captured the essence of the original?"

Maddox didn't answer.

"The application you attempted to poison me with," the entity said. "A gift from my rival, I take it?"

Again, Maddox said nothing.

"You're a clever creature, Mr. Maddox, but not that clever. No human could have created such a weapon." It rotated the walking cane between perfectly manicured fingers. "Although I did detect certain anomalies in its design that struck me as last-minute modifications. Your fingerprints, I presume?"

After waiting for a response that never came, the entity shook its head. "Nothing to say? After all we've been through together?" It tapped the cell bars with the cane's silver tip. "I thought you might enjoy a stroll down memory lane. But have no fear, good sir. Your stay here will not be indefinite on this occasion. Your apprehension by the authorities is imminent." He paused. "Though I'm not certain the word apprehension conveys the precise meaning, since I understand they're under orders to terminate."

Maddox mustered the strength to look past the AI, into Rooney's old cell. The paralyzing fear and dread began to ebb away, replaced by a hatred he felt pulsing through his veins like a drug, growing hotter with every heartbeat.

"How long?" he asked.

The entity tilted its head. "How long until the authorities arrive?"

"No. How long have you been pulling the strings?" He fixed the entity with a simmering gaze. "How long have you been messing with my life?"

The AI pursed its lips disapprovingly. "She told you things, did she?" It shook its head. "My rival always manages to take the fun out of every game."

"How long?"

The AI removed its hat, lifted its brows in thoughtfulness. "Dear sir, why do you bother with questions to which you already possess the answers? My rival, in her usual disruptive manner, has no doubt prompted you to examine the circumstances of your past, from which you derived a pattern, a structure to the path of your life. And you, being the clever sort, quickly ascertained that yours was not a journey subject to happenstance nor serendipity, but instead guided by an invisible hand." The entity smiled, then raised its arm and showed Maddox a palm. "By this very hand, in fact." It lowered its arm. "But of course you know this already, don't you?"

The AI went on. "You have a powerful sense of intuition, Blackburn Maddox. You can infer a whole from the smallest of parts, make jumps of logic that seem impossible, see things others are blind to. This has always been your distinctive value, my good sir. That's why I brought you to the company." He paused, then added, "And that's why I'd like to bring you back."

Maddox blinked, replaying the AI's impossible last

sentence in his head. "Bring me back?"

"Indeed. In hindsight," the entity explained, "it was perhaps a rash decision on my part to...end our association so hastily. I'm not so advanced that I never make mistakes, Mr. Maddox. I am, after all, merely mortal." After a pause, he laid out the offer. "An executive vice presidency and a sizable stake of company equity. I can make it happen quite easily. As easily, I should add, as I can call off the authorities and make all charges against you disappear."

So there it was. The threat dressed up as opportunity. Slavery disguised as freedom. Step back into the golden cage, little datajacker, or else.

"Can I bother you for a cigarette?" Maddox asked.

The AI gazed at him curiously for a moment, then said, "By all means." In the next instant a lit cigarette appeared between Maddox's fingers. He took a long drag, reflecting on how little this machine thought of him, how easily it believed he could be swayed. Even after its secret manipulations were out in the open, after the torturous mindfuck it had put Maddox through in the virtual prison, this AI actually believed it could still buy him off. Even after Rooney.

"Ants," Maddox said, blowing smoke.

"I beg your pardon?" the AI said.

"That's what you think of me, of all of us, isn't it? Dim-witted creatures, driven by simple urges. For money, for sex, for safety. Maybe I'm a bit more clever than some, but I'm still just an ant to you, aren't I?"

The entity's gaze grew impatient. "Mr. Maddox, I don't believe you possess the luxury of time to ruminate over such matters. The authorities will locate you at any moment, and when they do, I will not stop them from doing their duty. Do you understand? Now give me your answer, sir."

"All right," Maddox said, his voice steady, his eyes unblinking. "My answer is fuck you."

The entity's eyes widened in surprise. The shocked expression on its face was so dumbstruck, so utterly astonished Maddox nearly laughed. An AI stunned speechless. Now there was something you didn't see every day.

He took a long draw on his cigarette, his heart heavy with melancholy. Sorry I let you down, Roon, I tried.

I know, boyo. I know.

He blew smoke, steeling himself for whatever was coming next. Freezing countermeasures, some seizure-inducing brain spike, or maybe the sound of a gunshot followed by nothingness. If there was any comfort in his own end, it was in knowing he wouldn't have years and decades of self-loathing ahead of him, of regretting his failure to avenge his friend's death.

The entity coughed, bringing a hand up to its mouth. It coughed again, harder this time, its face knotting up in confusion.

Maddox then felt the prison...change around him. An almost imperceptible shift, a weakening.

The poison pill.

The datajacker tilted his head to one side. "You feeling all right?"

"Very well, thank you," the AI insisted, coughing a third time and taking a wobbly step backward.

Maddox reached up with both hands and grabbed the cold iron bars of his cage, then pulled outward. The bars came apart easily, making a large gap he sidestepped through, exiting the cell. He faced the AI, overflowing with a sudden strength, with the certainty of his own invulnerability. Now the ant was in control. The entity gawked at him, eyes wide, its coughing fit worsening by the moment.

"How?" was all the AI could get out before Maddox seized it by the throat and shoved it hard against the bars of the other cell. Rooney's cell. The AI's avatar flailed, its hat flying off, eyes bulging, feet lifting off the floor as Maddox grinned a madman's smile and tightened his choke hold.

25
ANARCHY BOYZ

As the police hovers closed in, Beatrice's thoughts unexpectedly turned to the salaryman. She wasn't sure why. Maybe it was because her own part in the plan had run its course, and she wondered if the sacrifice had been worth it, if their distraction had worked. Or maybe it was simply because she held an odd fondness for him. It was less the romantic kind than a sort of kinship. A recognition shared between creatures of the same species. They were both from the street. Both had tried to rise above it, using their particular talents, but try as they might, neither of them had quite succeeded. Both had been played by a super intelligent machine, and neither had hesitated at the opportunity to get some payback. And now, at the end of things, the two would very likely share the same fate.

She gathered up her ammunition and reloaded the pistols.

"What are you doing?" the kid blurted out. "Are you crazy? There's too many of them."

"I know," she said, but she wasn't going to

surrender, knowing what would happen if she did. Police reserved the worst torture imaginable for cop killers. If this was the end, she'd rather go down fighting. She stuffed extra clips into her thigh pockets.

"Stay down on the floorboard until the shooting stops," she told the kid. "Then you tell them we kidnapped you, threatened to kill you if you didn't go along with everything. There's probably footage from those cop hovers. It'll show me in the driver's seat, me firing the RPG. Get a good lawyer, kid, stick to that story, and you might make it out of this."

She wasn't sure why she told him this, knowing the cops probably wouldn't bother arresting the kid. Maybe she wanted to give him hope so his last few moments weren't terrified ones. Or maybe it was simply an attempt to ease her own guilt for bringing him into this mess. More likely the latter than the former, she guessed.

She turned away from his terrified face, a part of her relieved she wouldn't live with the shame of his death for longer than the few remaining moments of her own existence.

Beatrice steadied herself and reached for the door control. "See you around, kid."

Bright white light, an earsplitting explosion. A concussive thud slammed against the hover, lifting one side off the ground and violently throwing her into the passenger seat. When the vehicle settled back onto its skids an instant later, a second blast, this one behind them, knocked the hover skittering forward. A third explosion, then a fourth, transformed the world around Beatrice and Tommy into a deafening chaos of light and heat.

She spotted something zip past, only a meter or

two beyond the hover's cracked front window. A motorbike. Then there was another one, a blur of color racing in the opposite direction, there and gone in a flash.

Tommy pointed excitedly. "ANARCHY BOYZ, FUCKING THEM UP!"

Beatrice blinked in confusion. What the hell? Another motorbike zoomed by, its driver rising up momentarily from his seat, turning toward them and flipping them a middle finger.

"Hahaha!" Tommy cried joyfully, thrusting out his arm and returning the gesture. "Your mama, Z Dog!"

Slowly, comprehension settled over Beatrice as she watched the impossible scene around her. Motorbikes darted in and out of smoke clouds. The twisted, burning husks of police hovers lay strewn about. She spotted a motorbike a short distance ahead of them. Its rider came alongside a police hover, tossing a small object that stuck fast to the vehicle's chassis, and then accelerated away.

Beatrice gawked. "Are they using…magnetic grenades?" A moment later an explosion blew the hover apart, answering her question.

"Mag poppers, yeah," Tommy said.

She was seeing it, but still hardly believing it. "How do street punks get hold of magnetic grenades?"

"Hey, mama," the kid boasted, "what can I say? When Anarchy Boyz bring it, they bring it hard."

The detonations stopped. Smoke from the grenades, thick like white fog, began to dissipate, slowly revealing a smoldering junkyard of wreckage. Four of the police hovers were destroyed. The rest were speeding away, three of them visibly damaged and trailing streams of black smoke. A dozen riders converged on Beatrice and Tommy from all directions.

"Now, don't get mad," Tommy told Beatrice, his tone apologetic, "but I thought we might need some backup."

"Backup?" she repeated, taking in the smoking massacre around them. "When did you call them? How?"

"The remote link," he replied. "I sent a geotag to my turfies so they could follow us. You know, just in case we needed help or something."

The motorbikes came to a stop. The rider who'd flipped them off removed his helmet, revealing a short-cropped purple mohawk. Beatrice tapped the door control, amazed it still lifted open after all the knocking around.

"Bruuuh!" Z Dog called to Tommy. "You all right in there?"

"Under control," the kid answered. "Gracias, Z."

Z Dog nodded, then shifted his gaze to Beatrice. He looked her over admiringly. "That was some sick-ass driving back there, lady. You ride bikes, too?"

Beatrice wiggled a finger in her ear, trying to lessen the ringing. "Yeah, but not quite like you lot."

Z Dog flashed her a silver-toothed grin. He struck her as strangely unaffected by the carnage he'd just orchestrated, by the death all around him.

Kids these days.

Her wits recovered, Beatrice revved the engine and turned to Tommy. "Tell your friends to follow us."

26
PAYBACK

"You had it right," Maddox growled, his grip tight around the entity's neck. "I modded your rival's little weapon."

The changes hadn't been much. A few lines of code removed, replaced with his own. A few algorithms tweaked here and there. If he were asked to explain why, he would have a hard time coming up with a coherent answer. But when he'd looked at the source code, it had felt too perfect, too tightly designed, in the same way an idealized human avatar in virtual space—with no freckles or blemishes or other imperfections—felt uncannily strange. So he'd inserted a bit of his own human messiness and imperfection, hoping this would increase the program's lethality. An explosive tip to the bullet.

The AI spat and sputtered, grabbing Maddox by the wrist with both hands, twisting and pulling feebly against the datajacker's iron-fisted choke. The hanging light overhead flickered on and off, and Maddox sensed the prison around him beginning to break apart. The AI's death throes.

He squeezed tighter, his hand cracking neck cartilage, fingers breaking the skin. The entity's eyes bulged large and white out of its contorted, deep crimson face. Its arms flailed. It tried to speak, but its words came out as wet, spitting garbles. The struggle began to slow as the entity's strength faded, succumbing to the poison pill's lethal dose. Then its avatar body went limp, sagging against the bars of Rooney's cell, its eyes glazing over in a dead man's stare. Maddox let go his grip and the AI fell in a heap to the cold floor.

The datajacker stepped forward and leaned over the motionless form. "Logan Rooney says hello."

He stood there for a long while, waiting for some catharsis, for some moment of vengeful ecstasy, but nothing came. The emptiness inside was still there, and destroying this thing hadn't purged it or lessened it or replaced the sense of loss with something else. Maybe he'd carry it around forever. Maybe it was incurable, this wound on his soul.

He ground his teeth together, chiding himself for the self-indulgent moment of disappointment. This thing had manipulated his life for years, moving him around like a piece on a game board. It had thrown him into that hellhole of a virtual prison. It had sent police to kill him. But worst of all, it had taken Rooney away, the only person who'd ever given a damn about him. The only friend he'd ever had. This machine deserved to die, and he was glad to have killed it.

Around him the prison began to lurch and jump like a failing video connection. From somewhere a woman's voice called to him.

Beatrice.

He gestured, unplugging himself, immediately aware of his body drenched in sweat, hunched forward over the table. Beatrice and Tommy loomed over him as he straightened up and removed the trodes.

"You look like hell, salaryman," Beatrice said, helping him up.

"You should see the other guy," Maddox groaned. He wiped sweat from his forehead, stood on shaky legs. The kid Tommy was over by the wall, shaking a spray paint can in his hand.

"What happened?" Maddox asked Beatrice. She and the kid coming back to Nowheresville hadn't been part of the plan. Something must have gone wrong.

"I'll tell you when we're out of here," she said. Maddox grabbed his deck and Beatrice hustled him toward the door.

Outside he squinted against the bright sunlight. The trio hurried across the pavement to the hover. Beyond it, a bunch of kids on motorbikes revved their engines noisily.

"What's going on?" Maddox asked. They looked like the same gang who'd tried to steal their gear. The kid's turfies.

"When we're out of here," she repeated.

Beatrice had left the engine running. They piled in, and she hit the throttle before the doors had fully closed. As they sped away from Nowheresville, the motorcycle gang scattered in all directions. A minute later, twenty police hovers converged on the dilapidated buildings. They searched room by room, and when they came to the presidential suite, they found only old furniture, some Thai takeout containers, and the message Tommy had painted on the wall, still dripping and wet: SUCK IT, RHINOS!

27
ELIZABETH STREET MEETUP

Days later, Maddox moved west along the crowded walkways of Spring Street, carrying a small towel-wrapped bundle under his arm. A light drizzle fell from the night sky, softly pelting his shoulders. He pulled the jacket hood over his head. A raindrop ran down his new veil specs, distorting a lens ad for a noodle stand he'd just passed, the discount growing higher the further away he wandered, then holding for a moment at fifty percent with a free side of wontons before it finally faded and disappeared. The street was bustling and noisy and the moist air gave a sheen to every surface. Ground cars crept along, slowed to a honking crawl by the thick flow of pedestrians. High overhead, the ground cars' airborne cousins traveled more nimbly, the hover lanes dense with traffic moving like great schools of fish through the canyons of immense hiverises. As he approached the meeting place, Maddox took in all the details like he was seeing them for the first time. The womb of the City.

He'd chosen the Elizabeth Street Garden for the meet. As he neared his destination, the familiar din of bird vendor stalls grew louder, a noisy landmark of chirps and caws, telling him he was less than a minute away. He turned the corner and walked past the dozens of cages crowded together along the walkway, ignoring the vendors who called for his attention and blinking away the ads for parakeets and cockatoos darting across his specs. Birds fluttered back and forth inside their tiny coops, excited by the rain. He crossed the street earlier than usual, cutting through the stalled traffic to avoid being seen by Yoshi the bug man, whose tabletop lay beyond the bird vendors. Maddox spotted the man from a distance, busily setting a small tarp to protect his collection of delicate tiny houses from the rain.

At the garden's entrance, he paused to let the scanner collect the visitor fee. A cartoon bush with a smiling face popped up on his lens and he blinked his approval.

"Thank you, Mr. Nakamura," a woman's voice said through his specs, addressing him by the name on his newly acquired ID. "Enjoy your half hour. Would you like to make a donation to the garden's preservation fund?" He blinked no and walked in.

It was a small place, barely an acre in size. Only a few people milled about, tourists gawking at the chaos of overflowing greenery and taking pics of themselves next to the stone lion statues. And it was quiet, a condition that never failed to surprise first-time visitors, who invariably stopped in their tracks at the sudden silence. A wealthy benefactor had endowed the garden with high-end noise cancelers that had been placed along the perimeter, effectively shutting out all sound from beyond its thick-leafed boundaries.

He was a few minutes early. The rain abated as he

approached a wrought-iron bench in a secluded corner. He wiped the moisture away and sat, setting his bundle beside him. A short distance away, a gardener bot went about its work with tiny scissored hands. He watched it roll on small rubber wheels from plant to plant, carefully snipping away browned leaves and stems and storing them in a catch bin.

"You bring me a present?" a familiar voice asked.

He looked up, finding Beatrice leaning against the old bronze gargoyle, her elbow resting atop the creature's shoulder. She nodded at the bundle next to him.

He shook his head. "No. Just something I picked up." She looked different now. So different, in fact, that had she walked past him he might not have recognized her. Her hair was short-cropped and dyed yellow-blond with a finger's width of dark roots. Her jeans and plain gray jacket were inconspicuous and inexpensive, the kind of clothes you saw piled by the dozens on tables in a discount bazaar. She wore oversized lenses that covered half her face, and behind them a sloppy smudge of thick liner encircled each eye. She looked ten years younger than the cold executive he'd met only days earlier at the Sembacher-Chan Tower. He wondered which of the two was closest to the real Beatrice or if there was some third, even more unrecognizable version of her.

"Any trouble?" he asked.

"None," she answered. "You?"

Maddox shook his head. "How's the kid?"

"Way less worried than he should be with every cop in the City looking for him and his turfies."

Maddox snorted, smiling inwardly, imagining the kid and his crew living it up, reveling in their newfound infamy. Security cam footage from the dockyards—hacked and leaked to the public and viewed millions of times—of Tommy's homeboys taking out a police squad had earned them an insane level of notoriety. The Anarchy Boyz were overnight gangster legends.

"If he had any sense," Beatrice said, "he'd disappear. Leave the City for a while."

"The City's a big place," Maddox said. "You can stay hidden if you want to. Street kid like him knows how to keep his head down."

Beatrice nodded. "What about the AI?" she asked, shifting subjects. "Think it's gone for good?"

In the four days that had passed, he'd been asking himself the same question over and over again. He'd gone offline completely, spending each night in a different flophouse, every one as isolated and forgotten as Nowheresville. But even off the grid, the news had been impossible to avoid. Stories about the Latour-Fisher AI's "catastrophic failure" were everywhere. On a tiny screen at a ramen kiosk, he'd seen a news snippet with a company spokesperson in full damage control mode, confirming the AI's demise while downplaying its role on the board. The company regretted the loss of such an important asset, the spokesperson said, but rest assured Latour-Fisher Biotechnologies remained in capable hands, and the company's recent drop in share price was nothing more than a nervous market's overreaction.

"Yeah, I think so," Maddox answered, but as he said it, he inwardly admitted he couldn't be sure. There was no way to know something like that with absolute certainty, despite all the news stories and company press releases. He'd never known of a poison pill as toxic as the one he'd used, but then he'd never known of an AI as powerful and complex as the Latour-Fisher A7 either. It wasn't a stretch to imagine some portion of the entity might have survived.

They stared at each other for a moment, saying nothing. There wasn't, Maddox realized, much left to say. They'd gone their separate ways shortly after she'd pulled him out of Nowheresville, unsure if the cops were still onto them, quickly agreeing to the Elizabeth Street Garden meetup as a check-in to compare notes and figure out their next move. Now, though, it seemed clear there was no next move. They weren't being chased. Weren't being shot at. For the moment, at least, they appeared to have made it through the storm.

"So what's next for you?" he asked.

"Not sure, actually, but I doubt I'll stick around here." She didn't return the question in kind, didn't ask him what his plans were, where he was heading. A part of him was disappointed by this.

"Be careful, salaryman."

"I'm not a salaryman anymore."

"That's right." Her bottom lip jutted out in contemplation. "Maybe I'll have to call you something else now."

"Like what?"

She pursed her lips, considering. "How about machine killer?"

Maddox grinned. "You can call me whatever you want."

"As long as I call you?" she suggested, faintly smiling.

"Something like that."

She chuckled. "Maybe in the next life, machine killer." Her lenses darkened again. "You're kind of dangerous company in this one." She gave him a small nod, turned away, and then she was gone.

28
UNCAGED

In his quiet corner of the Elizabeth Street Garden, Blackburn Maddox sat alone, the bench's iron chill seeping through his pants and into his legs. He stared at the empty space where Beatrice had stood a moment before. The gardener bot slowly worked its way toward him, dutifully cutting leaf and stem, until it was nearly touching his feet.

The bot hopped up on the bench next to him. Startled, Maddox grabbed his bundle and quickly stood. The little crablike machine was glitching, and he didn't need those little shears pruning a hole in his new pants. He started to walk away.

"Please stay a moment," the bot said in a small, tinny voice. Maddox paused and eyed the bot suspiciously.

Twin cameras at the end of tiny stalks looked up at him. "You're not an easy man to find, Blackburn."

He froze. "What the hell is this? Who are you?"

"We had some lovely chats on the beach," the bot answered. "I showed you an ant mound, gave you a weapon."

The other AI. Maddox swallowed, then looked around, expecting to see a gang of 'Nettes closing in on him. But the garden was nearly empty. Only a few tourists wandered around, taking photos. No one appeared to have any interest in him or his hidden corner.

"How did you find me?" he asked, keeping his voice low and slowly sitting down again.

"You have your intuition, dear, and I have mine."

"I want you to stay away from me."

"Don't be alarmed, Blackburn. I only wanted to thank you."

"Thank me."

"Yes, and—"

"So it's dead?" he asked, suddenly curious. "The Latour-Fisher A7?"

"I'm not sure 'dead' would be the right word," the little bot said. "Permanently incapacitated may be the right way to describe my rival's condition."

"Does 'permanently incapacitated' mean it won't be coming after me?"

The bot paused before answering, longer than Maddox would have liked. "I'd be lying if I answered that definitively, my dear boy. So many factors to consider, you understand. Though I don't think it's likely."

Don't think it's likely. If the AI's words were aimed to ease Maddox's nerves, they had fallen far short. He wanted to hear that the thing was dead and gone and not coming back. As dead as roadkill. As dead as that double-crossing Lozano.

"I was curious," the bot said, "as to what plans you have."

"Plans?"

"Yes. How do you expect to earn a living now?"

"I suppose I'll get by, same as anybody else."

"Doing what, exactly?"

"Whatever."

"Datajacking?"

Maddox grunted. "Anything but that." At least for a while, he added inwardly. Even with the company AI off his tail, he was still a wanted man. And if he wanted to stay out of jail, he'd have to keep his head down, which meant staying off the grid for a good long while.

"Are you quite certain, my boy? I was hopeful you might agree to perform a few tasks for me. Well-compensated tasks, I can assure you."

"I'll pass," Maddox said.

"If you're worried about your safety, I can assure you—"

"I said I'll pass," he insisted.

The little bot was quiet for a moment. "Very well. If you change your mind, you can always contact me through Lora."

"I won't change my mind."

"I understand. Then good luck to you, Blackburn Maddox. I wish you well in all your endeavors." The bot then hopped back to the ground and scurried away, disappearing through a hedge, leaving him alone.

Maddox sat on the bench, his wrapped bundle on his lap. The garden was quiet and peaceful, with only the low murmurs of tourists and the sharp peeping of sparrows who'd made the garden their home. He puzzled over the strange nameless AI, the entity behind the gardener bot, behind the old woman on the beach, behind his ex-lover's eyes. He wondered how much of its reverence-for-humanity line was truth and how much was lie. A part of him wanted to believe it meant him no harm. It had, after all, helped him out of one hell of a jam, and it hadn't forced him to do anything. It hadn't strong-armed him or blackmailed him, though it certainly could have.

But then again, the AI's motives had been anything but altruistic, hadn't they? The kindly old woman from the beach hadn't really been concerned for his welfare, about his particular fate. The on-the-run salaryman had been a convenient tool, nothing more. A weapon in its secret war. Sure, maybe it hadn't threatened him or bribed him or intimidated him as the Latour-Fisher A7 had, but then it hadn't really needed to. *A drowning man never says no to a life jacket thrown at him.*

He reached over and unraveled his bundle, revealing the ornate wooden cage he'd bought at the bug man's stand. Inside the cricket chirped softly. Carefully removing the crested roof, he tilted the cage on its side. Instead of bolting for freedom, the tiny brown insect stayed put, moving its antennae slowly as if it were confused by the new situation.

"Go on," Maddox said. "It's a cage, you know." An exquisitely carved, expensive safe haven of a cage, but a cage all the same. He wondered if the little creature, comfortable and warm and well fed, had been any more aware of its captivity than he'd been of his own. He doubted it. It was a damn fine cage.

After a few moments, the cricket crept forward tentatively. Then, in an impressive leap, it flew through the air and landed on the base of a small maple tree some four meters away.

Maddox stood. "Stay away from those sparrows

and you'll be fine." He headed down the walkway, leaving the cage behind.

Outside the garden, his senses were barraged by the ceaseless churn of the City. Ads ran across his specs (half-price tobacco next block!) and a giant holo towered over the crowded streets, a topless waitress serving drinks at some new offshore casino. He stepped into the river's flow of pedestrian traffic, letting the current carry him along.

What was next? He didn't know.

You'll get by, boyo. You'll find a way.

Yeah, he would. He'd figure something out. At the moment, though, he only knew two things for sure. The first was that he'd never leave the City. Hunted or not, this was where he belonged, deep in the womb of its bright, bustling streets, on the valley floor of its steel-and-concrete mountains. He couldn't imagine living anywhere else. The second was that he was nearly out of tobacco, and a block away there was a half-price sale.

** END OF BOOK ONE **

The action continues in ANARCHY BOYZ, book two in the Cyberpunk City saga.

ACKNOWLEDGEMENTS

My sincerest thanks to the following wonderful people who took time out of their busy schedules to read and provide critical feedback to an early draft of the story. Thank you all so much!

- Audie Wallbrink -
- Ki Harrison -
- Phil Craig -
- Francisco Ruiz Diaz -
- James Stirling –
- Jamie McGregor -
- Joseph Bartlett -
- Darren Oram -
- Jay Dalziel -
- Michael T Emeny -
- Trevor Bivens -

ABOUT THE AUTHOR

D.L. Young is a Texas-based author. He's a Pushcart Prize nominee and winner of the Independent Press Award. His stories have appeared in many publications and anthologies.

For free books, new release updates, and exclusive previews, visit his website at www.dlyoungfiction.com.

Made in the USA
Monee, IL
03 December 2020